To Serena,
Enjoy the journey,
Blessings!
June Whatley

Trouble in Marrakesh

The Fine~Butterfly Detective Agency, Book 2

By June Whatley

Published by Gordian Books, an imprint of Winged Publications

This book is a work of fiction. Names, characters, places, and incidents are the product of the author's imagination and are used fictitiously. Any resemblance to actual events, locales, or persons, living or dead, is coincidental.

ISBN: 978-1-956654-29-5

Dedication:

I wholeheartedly dedicate this book to Kay Wojack, my dear friend and *partner in crime*, as her husband calls us. Through thick and thin she has believed in me and spurred me onward. If not for her, this book would probably never have been written. Her occasional question of what would be next for the ladies of *The Fine~Butterfly Detective Agency,* pressed me forward.

Kay is also my chief Beta Reader and offers excellent suggestions. With a smile on my face, I write, she already wants to know what's next for the ladies. She wants them back stateside, in their fictitious hometown that I may call Garden City. What better place for a Fine~Butterfly?

We will have to wait and see if the Lord provides more inspiration for me as the writer and more intrigue for the sisters.

All I can say is, Praise the Lord!

Outline

Chapter 1

The Renovated House

The family watched as Abigail turned the knob at the front entrance of her home, the door swung in as smooth as silk, sunlight flooding the beautiful marble entryway. She lifted her foot to step inside. "I can't wait to see it!"

Sam grabbed her by the arm. "Wait just a minute, little lady, you can't go in there."

Her head whipped his direction and large eyes stared back at him. "Why not? Anthony said it's finished."

He leaned his face close to hers. "Because, you've never crossed that threshold as the lovely Mrs.-Doctor Abigail Fine-Fielding before." He smiled and scooped Abby's petite frame into his arms as she giggled. "Now, we'll cross it together." He stepped through the doorway and carried her from the foyer, into the living room, followed by their familial entourage.

With her arms wrapped securely around his neck, she kissed his cheek. "You, big sweetie," she grinned, then swished her legs, "now put me down."

When her feet touched the floor, she turned to survey the work that George's grandson and his crew had done to her home over the past month, her hands sprang to her cheeks with a light slap.

Tony stepped in beside her. "Well, what do you think, Aunt Abby?"

With her mouth wide open, she faced him, then managed to mutter, "Oh, Anthony, dear, it looks marvelous. You've totally changed everything." She turned to face the back of the room. "What do you call this wonderful wall color? It's absolutely divine."

"That's the newest trend in home interiors, it's called Deep Mediterranean Blue."

"I love it, dear, I simply love it, it makes the white sofa, marble floor and satin trim stand out beautifully."

He placed his hand on her arm and tugged. "Now, come look at the kitchen, Aunt Abs."

She walked to the door and threw both hands over her mouth, then they slid to her chest. "Oh Samuel, come look at this, it's stunning."

Sam entered behind Abby and flashed a smile at Anthony. "Well, done, nephew. I'm no expert or anything, but this looks terrific."

Sparkling stainless steel handles set-off the dark blue cabinets. The countertop gleamed brightly under the cut-glass light fixture which hung where the parrot had once dangled.

"I hoped you'd like it, Aunt Abs. I took a similar approach for the colors in here, see the cabinets are finished in the same deep Mediterranean-color, but with a finish slightly flatter than the living room walls, then topped with a glaze and I used stainless steel for the accessories and appliances. I mirrored the sofa color on the backsplash and in the white and gray marbled countertop, the floor is the same marble tile throughout the foyer, living room, dining room and kitchen."

"Oh, Anthony, it's splendid. It's so bright and fresh, I love everything about it." Abby lifted her voice. "Millie, you and George have to come see this."

Millie plodded into her sister's once-drenched kitchen, followed by her new husband.

George surveyed the work his grandson had done. "Oh, my goodness, Tony, you've done a wonderful job. This is amazing."

"Thanks, Gramps." He put on an impish grin and leaned toward Millie. "What do you think, Granny?"

Millie made a face in gest. "That'll be enough out of you, Cheeky Monkey, you call me Millie, that will do just fine."

He tossed his hands out to his sides. "But honestly, you need some kind of title," he spread his hands as if reading a marquee, "like G-momma. What about that?"

She faced George and smiled at her new husband, but directed the remark at Tony. "Mrs. George Williams is all the title I need, sweetie."

George pulled her shoulder to his chest. "You are quite a woman, my Mildred Butterfly-Williams."

Tony suddenly walked to the far corner of the room and pulled a sheet from where it hung. "Ta-da!"

A squawk filled the kitchen, followed by, "Avast ye, Mateys."

Abby squealed, "Black Beard!"

Millie hooted, "The old booty-biter himself."

Perched on a swing in a new stainless-steel cage, the parrot cocked his head and glared at them.

Abby walked toward the cage, but glanced back at

Anthony. "Oh, honey, thanks for taking such good care of him. He looks wonderful, so sleek and shiny."

Tony laughed. "Well, we couldn't have a dirty bird, littering up the place, could we? I gave him a shower this morning at my place before bringing him home." He chuckled. "Now everybody, let's go check-out the office."

The group reversed direction and passed through the living room into what Millie had formerly referred to as 'the swamp.' Wide, white blinds let in the sun, the Mediterranean blue walls and bright white carpet, off-set the large mahogany desk and file cabinet.

Abby slowly revolved in the room to take in every inch. "Anthony, sweetheart, you got rid of all the old drab paint and that awful wallpaper border. This looks stunning too."

He winked at her. "Just right for you and G'Millie to setup your new detective agency."

A familiar belly-laugh erupted from beside Abby. "I'm not sure Abigail and I are up to that, but the room is lovely, Tony dear."

George's eyes narrowed and he glanced around the group. "This is as good a time as any for a formal, family discussion, would everyone join me in the living room?"

Four sets of eyes darted back and forth, but everyone followed George.

Sam, Abby and Millie parked themselves on the sofa.

Tony plopped down in one of the comfy chairs. "What's up, Gramps?"

George lowered himself onto the arm of the chair opposite his grandson. "Jeremiah received a message from Interpol, they're requesting that Millie come to Marrakesh, Morocco, to testify against Ferdinand in the case regarding the theft of the yacht. If she doesn't appear as a witness, his confession to her will be considered as hearsay evidence." He looked at his wife. "Having you testify will be the only leverage they have to force Ferdinand to name the scoundrels he worked with." George stuffed his hands in his pockets. "Millie, are you up to this?"

She leaned forward. "Well, if I don't go, will he get off scot-free?"

"Maybe not scot-free because some of the crew members will testify that he told them to set-sail, after which he was nowhere to be found, but most likely he will get a light sentence. The problem is not only that, some of the crewmen who were set adrift, suffered injury due to the intense sun and dehydration. Those dirty hijackers set them out in the lifeboat without water and on an outgoing tide. Moroccan law enforcement wants the names of the thieves who boarded the yacht and the ringleader who gave the orders."

Millie gasped and her hands flew up from her lap. "That does it! I'm in. How do we arrange this?"

George smiled. "That's my girl! Interpol will handle the travel details through Jeremiah, now here's the second part of the discussion. Since the Chief Mate of the *Princess of the Sea* is in custody for kidnapping you, Millie, and because he was supposed to take command of the new ship, *Princess of the Med*, that means Jeremiah will have to take command of the new boat and his new second-in-command will take the helm of the original *Princess*."

Anthony bent his elbows and placed his hands

behind his head. "Is that what Dad wants to happen, Gramps?"

"Well, Tony-boy, it wasn't his first choice, but he's put in a few special requests. Number one is for your mother to be allowed to travel with him and that's been approved. He's also put in a request for some special crewmembers to ease the transition." He shifted his glance to Sam. "He's going to need a doctor and he wants you to take the position."

Abby pushed forward and bristled. "But we just got married last night!"

George laughed. "Taking that into consideration, Abby, how would you like to honeymoon on a Mediterranean cruise."

Her eyes brightened, her shoulders rose, she grabbed her husband's arm and smiled at him. "Oh, Sam, doesn't that sound romantic?"

He patted her hand but looked at George. "So, you're sure they're going to allow Abby to sail with me? And will that be a permanent arrangement?"

"Whenever you are required to be aboard, she's welcome. Since she'll share your room and," he winked at her, "we know she eats very little, she'll travel free, but of course, that means no pay raise for you and if you fly back and forth to the states, you two will have to pay your own airfare."

Sam looked at his wife's smiling face, then back at George. "Sounds great! We'll take it."

"Okay, but you'll need to be ready to meet the ship during her last month of preparation, to stock the infirmary and make sure it's *ship-shape*, so to speak." George smiled. "Sam, can you be ready to leave in a month? Abby can fly over with us when we travel."

They all looked at Abby who smiled at Sam and nodded, yes.

George scanned the four people in the room. "Good! Now another concession he asked for involved Shelly and Rebecca. That one's already been approved and the girls can't wait. They'll leave in a month to set-up and stock the beauty salon and I would appreciate it, Sam, if you would travel with them."

Sam nodded and swung his arm around Abby's shoulder. "Sure thing, I wouldn't want the girls to travel alone."

George's gaze shifted back to his grandson. "Now for you, Tony."

He sat up straight and smiled. "Yes, sir?"

"Your dad wants you to join the team as the head of the maintenance crew. New ships always need some tweaking when they first set out, but it'll require that you put your construction company into someone else's hands while you're away and you'll have to be ready to go to Turku, Finland, in three days. If you take the job, you'll travel with your dad to join the builders in the last two months of prep, so, what do you say?"

"Wow, that came out of the blue, Gramps, but," he paused, "I don't want to be here if the rest of the family's in the Mediterranean. Let me talk to my guy, Jeff Collins and see if he's up to taking the lead with the crew. Give me a minute." He stood, pulled his cell phone from his pocket and turned toward the office.

George continued. "The rest of us will have to make arrangements to close up our homes and fly to Tangier, Morocco, in two months. The Med cruises last three months so there'll be a lot to do before we go." He turned to Abby. "Do you think you remember how to make coffee?" and grinned.

"Okay, Mr. Smarty Pants, of course I remember how to make coffee. Follow me to the kitchen and learn a few things."

Millie stood with her. "He's Mr. Cranky Pants, remember?" And she flashed a smile at her grinning husband.

A welcoming aroma wafted from the kitchen, as Anthony entered the room chuckling.

George pushed his cup away from his lips. "What's up, Tony?"

"Well, Gramps, it seems that God is in control. Collins told me he was on the verge of quitting because he wanted a job with more challenge and more money, so I gave him the lead position with the crew and gave him a raise. When I told him I'd be going out of the country for an indefinite length of time, he asked me if he could take over the lease on my apartment? Turns out he's getting married in a week and needs a better place. We agreed that I'll still get a small percentage of the profit of the company, since I'm the founder and might be back to step-in again sometime in the future."

Millie's belly-laugh filled the room. "Praise the Lord, he's always in control, we just sometimes forget to realize it. Anthony, sweetie, we'll help you pack and anything that needs to go into storage can be put in one of the bays of your dad's garage."

George smiled. "Our garage, Millie."

Anthony waved his hand. "Actually, he wants the furniture and all the household dishes, pans and linens too. He said he'd pay me a grand for the whole lot. All I have to pack is my personal stuff and clothes. I couldn't have asked for a better deal. We'll go to the landlord tomorrow and make it official and Gramps, can I stay with you and G'Millie a couple of days while I arrange to fly out?"

Another laugh erupted from Millie. "I'm sure we can find room for you in one of the six bedrooms, sweetie."

Abby's eyes widened. "Six bedrooms?"

Millie nodded. "Yes, George has quite a mansion, six bedrooms, eight bathrooms, a separate maid's quarters, a living room, dining room, kitchen and I haven't even seen what's behind some of the doors." She laughed again. "I almost got lost at one point."

Everyone laughed.

Chapter 2

Three Days Later

Jeremiah's wife Sally stood, with their two daughters Shell and Becca, behind the barrier at the airport, waving goodbye and blowing kisses to her husband and son Anthony. She turned to her father-in-law George, "Dad, I can't believe they're really leaving for Finland. Have we made the right decision?"

George stepped close and placed his arm around her shoulder. "I'm sure everything will be fine."

She wiped tears from her face. "But in a month the girls will leave with Sam and I'll be alone, again."

Millie stepped next to George. "Sally, you can close your house up early and come stay with us. We wouldn't mind at all, would we George?"

George placed his other arm around his wife. "Of course, she can stay with us! Sally, we don't want you to be alone. After we see Shell, Becca and Sam off next month, we will help you pack what you need for the cruise, then we can cut your utilities and you can stay with us until we leave."

Sally sniffled. "I don't want to be a burden."

Millie came around and faced her. "Nonsense! You could never be a burden. You're the daughter I always wanted, but never had until this family welcomed me in. Now it's settled, you will stay with us."

Shell and Becca leaned in and gave a group hug. "Thanks Gramps and G'Millie, you two are the best."

Becca looked at her mom. "I hadn't said anything, but I was worried about you being alone the month before you fly to Morocco. Dad had never been gone for more than a month and when we were home it wasn't so bad, but when Shell and I joined the crew and Tony got his own apartment, we could tell a difference in you, even when we were home for the weekend, we could tell you dreaded the thought of us leaving again on Monday."

Sally dried her face and hugged her daughters. "Being totally alone in that big, old house didn't agree with me. I couldn't believe how much I missed you all."

Millie stepped back. "It's settled then, when the girls leave, you are moving in with us." She turned to face her sister and Sam. "And would you feel better if Abby moved in with us too?"

Sam's shoulders relaxed, he looked into the face of his precious bride. "Actually, I would feel much better. I know that Abby had been on her own for a while, but then you moved in with her, Millie. I can tell from the way she talks about the past that she didn't enjoy being by herself. You were a God-send for her."

A smiled widened across Millie's face. "It was mutual Sam, I needed her as much as she needed me." Then she looked at George. "I guess I should have cleared this with you, dear, before filling your house with these scoundrels."

George laughed and pulled her in close. "As long as you are one of the scoundrels who fills *our house*, it'll be just fine with me," and sealed it with a long, passionate kiss.

Chapter 3

One Month Later

Standing behind the barricade again, this time Abby, armed with a lace handkerchief and Sally waved goodbye to Sam, Becca and Shell.

As their loved ones disappeared down the corridor, Millie stepped forward and placed an arm around Abby and Sally. "Come on girls, let's get you all packed up and moved into the house with George and me."

Abby blew her nose on the lace hanky. "Sam made sure I was packed before he left. I couldn't believe he didn't want me to spend even one night by myself."

Millie cackled. "He's already learned what a procrastinator you are."

Abby swatted the air next to her sister. "Oh, Millie, you know I'm not that bad."

Millie's eyebrows arched and she chucked. "Uh-huh!"

Abby added, "Oh, and thanks for having your house-sitter watch Black Beard. I'm sure he will be happier there than he would be onboard the ship, even though it was sweet of Jeremiah to okay it."

Sally turned toward them. "Well, I'm ready too. All of my clothes for the cruise are packed and the girls helped me clean out the refrigerator last night. All that's left is to turn off the power, water and cable."

George joined them. "That's wonderful. We'll put all the utilities on hold indefinitely, drain the water lines and you'll be able to get your final bills before we leave. We'll alert your Neighborhood Watches to keep an eye on things."

Sally placed her hands on her cheeks. "I never realized how this would feel. Should we have put our houses on the market to sell it? Even when we come back we'll have to take a couple of days to turn everything on again."

Millie's mouth flew open. "I hadn't thought about that, Sally. You and Abby could be gone for a year before you fly back home." She turned to George. "Honey, had you thought about that?"

He smiled at his wife. "Yes, dear, Jeremiah, Sam and I had a confab about it. Jeremiah decided not to sell. He may be looking at retirement in five years and Sam didn't feel that he had any right to suggest such a thing to Abby since it's her house, so we all stayed quiet. Besides, Sam is only doing this for Jeremiah. When he retires, they both will, I'm sure. All Jeremiah and Sam will have to do is contact the utility companies a few days before coming home and set a date to restart service, it's not a big deal."

She leaned on his shoulder. "I'm so glad that we have husbands with good heads on their shoulders." She glanced at her sister whose face looked tight. "What's wrong, Abigail?"

"I didn't know how Sam felt about the house. It never crossed my mind that he might not feel at home in a place I'd shared with Henry."

George placed his hand on her arm. “It’s not that at all, Abby. He just didn’t feel that he had a right to discuss selling a home that you had owned before he came into your life, but I assure you he’s been very content there. The two of you may not come back to the states but once a year, but he’s happy to have your place, or is it your two’s place, aww heck, y’all’s house to come back to.”

The four of them laughed.

Chapter 4

Another Month Flew By

The foursome stood at a tall table in the airport coffee bar, waiting for their flight.

Millie turned to George. "I'm glad you got a house-sitter instead of closing up our place."

"Well, we might not be gone as long as everyone else. They all have jobs," he peered across the table at Sally and Abby, "or husbands, on the ship, but when you're finished testifying, we can either stay with the Med cruise for three months or fly home immediately. I'll leave it up to you to decide."

"I'm not sure I want that responsibility, George."

"Millie, I just meant if you are too tired to continue, I'll gladly get us tickets to fly home. Neither of us knows the impact this trial will have on you."

"I'm sorry, George, I just like for you to make decisions for me." She leaned in and squeezed his arm. "You're so good at it. I loved Max, but I had to make every decision that was ever made about the house, travel, what we ate—everything." She smiled into space, "but the man made me feel so loved." She looked back at George. "Just like you do, dear, but now I feel like I'm on vacation all the time when I'm with you. I can't believe you love me."

George took her in his arms. “Are you still certain you’re up to testifying at this trial?”

“Yes, I’ve prayed about it. I feel like it won’t be easy, but it’s the right thing to do.”

“You amaze me, my beautiful lady!” He kissed her.

A scolding voice streamed across the table, “Hey, you two, that’s enough of that sweet stuff.” Jeremiah’s wife laughed. “I’m not with my man yet.”

Abby giggled. “Yeah, cut it out, we don’t have our husbands.”

Millie laughed. “Okay, we’ll stop, for a little while anyway. I can hardly believe Anthony and Jeremiah have been gone two months already and Sam and the girls have been gone for one, but here we stand at the airport, my goodness, how time’s flown by.”

The loudspeaker crackled. “The plane for Tangier, Morocco, is now boarding at Gate Three.”

George smiled. “Coffees down ladies, our new lives await.”

Onboard the plane, Millie and George settled into their seats. Across from them, in the center aisle, Abby and Sally chatted away. George turned to his wife and smiled. “This is the best family on earth.”

Millie leaned into his shoulder. “Indeed, they are, we’re blessed beyond measure, my love.”

Chapter 5

Arrival in Morocco

The plane landed with a bounce and an *eeek* of the tires, then rolled to a smooth stop. Outside on the tarmac, attendants raced to position metal stairs beneath the hatchway just before the flight attendant opened the door.

With carry-on bags in hand, the passengers proceeded to the door and made their way down the steps.

Inside the terminal, Tony shouted to them from behind a barricade. "Welcome to Tangier, I've missed you all so much!"

After they passed through customs, George, Millie and Abby watched as Tony flung his arms around his mother and kissed her on the cheek, then hugged Abby. At Millie he stopped and looked her straight in the eyes. "G'Millie, I never thought there would be anyone who could step into my grandmother's shoes, but you fill them very well."

She pulled him in for a hug. "Sweetie, I could never take Shelly's place, but I'm so happy this family has welcomed me in. You're the best family on earth." She glanced over at her husband and smiled. "Your Gramps and I had already decided that on the plane."

George grabbed his grandson, clapped his hand onto his back and pulled him in for a hug. "And you, Tony-boy, helped me set the snare for this wonderful *butterfly*." A Cranky Pants-type *he-he-he* erupted from him, causing the family to laugh and people nearby to stare.

Tony grinned. "And when we netted the *butterfly*, Gramps, I didn't know we would also catch a *fine* specimen for Uncle Sam too." He looked at Abby and smiled.

She swatted the air toward his arm. "Oh, Anthony, you're so sweet."

He backed away from George and smiled. "We'd better get you all to the ship or dad will send out a search party." He held out his hand in the open-palmed, Princess-style gesture pointing the way.

Half an hour later, when their car pulled onto a short pier, a small boat waited.

"The port here is too shallow to allow the *Princess of the Med* to dock." Anthony pointed, "We'll take the water taxi to the ship and board from a floating dock."

The trip took only minutes, the *Princess of the Med* glistened in the Tangier sun as it rested in the beautiful Mediterranean water.

George beamed with pride as they approached.

Topside, Jeremiah and Sam leaned on the rail, then rushed down the angled gangway to help their ladies onto the small, bobbing platform next to the ship.

Jeremiah took Sally's hand and helped her step over the rail, then embraced her. "Oh my, how I've missed you."

Sam extended his arm toward Abby. "Come here, gorgeous."

She giggled and took Sam's outstretched hand, stepped onto a cushioned seat, then over the rail onto the floating dock.

As the taxi captain held the mooring rope as tight as possible, George helped Millie to traverse the side of the boat, then he scrambled onto the floating platform behind her. To prevent causing turbulence, the water taxi captain waited for the passengers to climb the stairs before turning his small vessel back toward shore.

When they arrived topside, Jeremiah looked at his dad. "Thank you for getting all of these lovely ladies here safely."

George took his son's hand, but rather than shaking it, he pulled him in for a hug. "Son, it's so good to see you. You look fantastic." He scanned the deck of the *Princess*. "And the ship is absolutely beautiful."

Jeremiah grinned, turned to view his new vessel and patted his dad on the back. "Let's get you settled, is anyone hungry and you probably all need to get some rest before you take a tour."

Chapter 6

A Warm Reunion

With Sally clutching his arm and pressing into his shoulder, Jeremiah escorted his family to the dining hall where Shell and Becca waited. Their voices blasted rapid-fire toward the open door.

"Momma!"

"Gramps!"

"G'Millie!"

"Aunt Abby!"

They rushed forward and arms flew around bodies in welcoming hugs.

Becca shouted, "It's so good to see you all. We've never been so glad to see anyone in our lives. We've missed you all tremendously!"

Shell added, "Yeah and now maybe Dad and Uncle Sam will stop being so gloomy."

Laughter burst out all around, including from Jeremiah and Sam.

Becca motioned toward a table and led the way. "Since we won't be picking-up passengers for a couple of days, we've requested family-style meals from the chef. We've set the table and I'll let him know that we're ready."

Shell chuckled as she arrived with a tray of glasses

of sweet tea. "And I can tell you, it was a chore to teach him how to make *this* delicacy, he would serve wine with breakfast if we'd let him."

The thought caused laughter all around again.

The chef served a scrumptious meal of shrimp in a rich, white sauce over linguini, accompanied by a Greek salad and soft garlic bread knots, while slices of a mysterious date and nut cake waited on a cart to the side.

Jeremiah took a moment to describe his experience with the building of the ship. "When Anthony and I arrived in Turku, Finland, the ship was merely a shell with an engine room in the belly. We watched day-after-day, as they lowered completed rooms into the hull and locked them into place; walls, beds, bathrooms and closets were intact in each unit and placed in position like puzzle pieces. After the puzzle was completed for the crew deck, Anthony and I thought we could move into our rooms, but early every morning the deafening sound of machinery echoed inside like an empty tin can, so we were forced back into our luxury hotel." He chuckled and glanced at his dad, "Honest, Cranky Pants, we tried to save money."

Laughter exploded from the group.

Following lunch, rooms were discussed, Jeremiah gestured and Porter Robbie Ferguson scurried alongside to help George and Millie.

Millie grinned. "Robbie, son, what are you doing on the *Princess of the Med*?"

The boy beamed. "Mrs. Millie," he glanced at Jeremiah and nodded, "when Captain Williams asked for volunteers to be uprooted from the Caribbean, my mom and I jumped at the chance to join his new crew."

"That's wonderful, dear, how's your mother?"

"She's doing great, ma'am. Doc Fielding arranged for her ankle to be operated on under ship's insurance and she can walk normal again. Meeting you was the most wonderful thing that ever happened to us, Mrs. Millie. We both thank you very much!"

"You need to thank the Lord, Robbie, not me."

He nodded. "Oh, yes ma'am, we do. Mom's a Christian now too because of what you did for me. I could have been in jail now, instead of working on this sweet ship." Grinning broadly, he announced, "If we were Catholic, I'd tried to have them make you a Saint."

Millie tossed her head back and belted out a laugh that echoed in the dining room. "Come here you rascal and give your spiritual mom a big hug."

George laughed too. "I'd vote, yes, on Sainthood with you, Robbie."

The young porter held out his hand in the cruise ship-style manner, to show them the way to their room. Once there, he swiped the metal keycard across the pad next to their cabin door and handed the card to George. "Mr. Williams, this is quite a lady you have for a wife."

"I totally agree, Robbie." George leaned over and kissed his wife on the cheek. "After you, my dear." His hand slid smoothly through the air in a captain-like manner.

She stepped across the threshold and gasped, as she slapped her hands to her face. "I thought the *Princess of the Sea* stateroom was gorgeous, but this is absolutely glamourous."

A light blue silk comforter shimmered as the sun streaked through the patio door. A deep Mediterranean blue satin throw rested casually across the foot of the bed. Wallpaper with a silvery, metallic sheen accented the wall behind the bed and was flanked by crystal lamps on each nightstand. Drapes, marbled with streaks of light and deep blues, swaged at each end of the glass doors. The sky and sea hues from outside made striking companions for the curtains and comforter, causing the whole space to be gracefully extended onto the patio which was dressed with two stainless steel chairs and a small round table, a matching rail just beyond outlined the scene.

"George darling, this is …"

"Yes, dear?"

"I don't know, George, I'm afraid to move. I'm afraid it might all vanish in a mist."

George laughed, turned her to face him and wrapped his arms around her. "Then hang onto me, I won't let it disappear, my love."

She hugged him and laid her head on his shoulder. "I will cling to you from now on, George. I had a great marriage to Max and when I lost him, I thought I'd never be truly happy again, then you swept into my life. You haven't erased him, you just carved out a whole new place in my heart that no one could fill, but you, I'm the most blessed woman that's ever lived."

From behind her, through the open door, a familiar voice drifted into the room. "Then I must be the second most blessed woman who ever lived."

Millie lifted her eyes over George's shoulder, he turned and said, "Abby, Sam, come in."

Millie strolled toward her sister. “Oh, Abigail, isn’t this lovely? What’s your suite like?”

Abby grinned. “Not nearly as nice as yours, dear, but it has one amenity that I can’t live without.” She beamed up at Sam. “The doctor and I are cozily ensconced in a very nice little room on the crew deck, but I find it to be the most romantic and charming room I’ve ever known.”

The corners of Millie’s mouth drooped. “Oh, honey, it never crossed my mind that you’d be on the crew deck. Are there any little luxuries that I can smuggle down to you?”

“No, truly, I’m as happy as clam in our little shell.” She smiled at Sam again, then glanced back at Millie. “You know that Henry was wonderful to me, but I’ve never felt so content in my life. This man has become the light of my world,” her eyes flashed back to her sister, “second only to the Lord, you understand.”

Millie laughed. “Sam, did you give her some more of that wonderful medication you supplied her with when I was kidnapped?”

Abby gave the air another swat. “Oh Millie, do be serious.”

“I’m sorry, dearest. I’m thrilled that we’re both so happy and Sam you are a treasure, we both love you.” She cut her eyes over to George. “And you too, Cranky Pants.”

They all laughed, but George wrapped his arms around her again. “We’re all blessed, my dearest lady.”

Chapter 7

The Briefing

After some rest, Jeremiah escorted his family around the ship. "This *Princess* is much smaller than her Caribbean sister, but she's a delight. On our way from Finland, we traveled through the English Channel, then around Portugal and Spain." He glanced at George. "She handles like a dream, Dad, so streamlined and maneuverable. We landed here off the coast of Tangier to await your arrival. Tomorrow we'll work our way through the Strait of Gibraltar and on to the port of Tangier Med, where most of our travelers will board in two days." He stopped and turned to address his dad and Millie. "I'm afraid we'll have to drop Millie off here in Tangier to catch the train to Casablanca, then another on to Marrakesh, there's no direct train from here to the final destination."

George's hands flew up. "But son, we just got here."

Jeremiah shook his head. "I know dad, but the prosecutor wants to see Millie as soon as possible to prep her for the trial. The Tribunal is scheduled to start Wednesday." He directed his gaze at Millie. "You can get a good night's sleep tonight on the ship and we'll get you an escort to the train station tomorrow morning."

Abigail held Sam's arm. "Oh no, Millie that's too soon and I don't want you to travel alone."

George joined in her sentiment. "Wow, I agree, that was fast, son and we can't let her go alone, but you know that I have Board of Directors' Meetings for the next two days while we travel to Tangier Med."

"I know, Dad, I didn't want to worry you with the time schedule. I figured it would be a little tight, but still very doable."

Sally smiled at her husband. "Honey, maybe you could talk to the prosecutor into giving her a day or two to catch her breath, then she could stay on board all the way to the next port and catch the direct train from there."

Millie weighed in. "No, this is fine. At least I don't have a lot of time to sit around and think about it. I'd rather get to it and get it done."

George smiled and gripped her hand. "You're amazing, Millie, I love you so much."

"Thanks, sweet man! I love you too. Now perhaps we should sample some of the chef's amazing dinner. We don't want him to have a temper tantrum."

Jeremiah laughed and extended his hand. "This way, Millie, I hear that tonight is a special treat of Sirloin Tip Roast, a rare feast in the Mediterranean area. It's not like back home where beef's in abundance, I can hardly wait to sink my teeth into it."

At dinner, the family chatted away as they consumed the main course, plus roasted potatoes, Green Beans Almandine and luscious slices of chocolate cake.

The chef came tableside to see if everything was

agreeable.

Millie grabbed his hand between hers and patted it. "It was wonderful, thank you for all of your attention to the details. You are a true artiste."

He smiled as if the Queen of England had complimented him. "You are most gracious, Madame Millie." He bowed, then wheeled toward the kitchen.

Jeremiah leaned on his elbows. "Millie, you've made a friend. That's the first time I've seen Jean Claude smile since he came aboard. You have a real knack with people."

George patted her shoulder. "Yes, she does, son! Yes, she does."

After dinner, Jeremiah was speaking to his father and Millie about a young man who could escort Millie to the train station, when Abigail walked up, pushed her shoulders back and tipped her chin. "Millie, Sam and I have agreed that it's too dangerous for you to travel alone, even with an escort." She puffed out her chest. "I'll be traveling with you, Sam and I have decided."

Millie's eyes widened. "But honey, that's not necessary."

Sam leaned in. "No use arguing, Millie, Abby has her mind made up."

A young man stepped from the kitchen, Jeremiah gestured his direction. "Dad, this is Jean Claude's son, Bastien."

The lad nodded to the group, then extended his hand. "Hello, Mr. Williams, it is a pleasure to meet you." He smiled as he withdrew his hand from George's and turned to Millie. "And Mrs. Williams, I must say that you—charming lady, have made quite an impression on my father and if you wish, I will accompany you all the way to Marrakesh to make sure your connections and accommodations are suitable. My father says he can spare me from the kitchen for a couple of days and has instructed me to take exquisite care of you."

Millie grinned. "Thank you for the offer, Bastien, tell your father, merci beaucoup, but I'm sure we will be fine. My sister will be traveling with me."

He bowed and headed for the kitchen.

Jeremiah pointed the way for his dad and Millie and as they walked he said, "You know, Millie, it might be a good idea to accept his offer. There are some street thieves and pickpockets in Morocco."

George looked at him with concern, but she waved her hand. "Pish posh, tourist travel here all the time and are fine. I'm sure you're being overly cautious."

Jeremiah leaned in. "I have a feeling, Millie, that's all. You are too precious to us to take any chances."

She patted his cheek. "Son, you are sweet to be concerned, but I'm sure Abby and I will be fine. The sooner we leave, the sooner this will be finished."

They reached the stateroom and Millie gave Jeremiah a hug. "What time should we prepare to leave?"

"Breakfast will be at seven and the train leaves at half-past eight. Pack yourselves bags for a few nights' stay and let us know when you get settled. I've made reservations for you at El Fenn Hotel in Marrakesh."

George hugged his son, then entered the room with Millie. As the door closed behind them, he turned his wife to face him and stared into her eyes. "Millie, Jeremiah rarely overreacts to anything, I think you and

Abby should take Bastien up on his offer. It would help me to sleep easier."

"Oh, George, dear. I'm sure we'll be fine." But she suddenly saw something in his eyes that she'd not seen before, not fear exactly, but foreboding. "Very well, darling, if it would help you rest easier, I'll agree."

George crossed the room to the phone and called Jeremiah's cell number. "Son, we've discussed it and Millie would welcome Bastien's company on their trip. Would you ask him to pack for a round trip journey to Marrakesh?"

Even Millie, could hear the sigh of relief through the phone's receiver. "That's great, Dad, I certainly feel better. I'll let Sam and Abby know too. Goodnight, Dad, I love you!"

George smiled and replied. "Goodnight, son, love you too."

Millie shouted, "Goodnight son! I love you too," and smiled.

Chapter 8

At Breakfast

Jeremiah greeted his dad, Millie, Abby and Sam. "I have tickets for the ladies and Bastien to Casablanca, then on to Marrakesh and I've notified Saunders of your arrival this afternoon so he can meet you. Bastien is collecting the bags now, so you need to eat breakfast."

Millie bristled. "Bastien needs some breakfast too, Jeremiah."

He crossed his arms and rested his hands on his biceps. "Not to worry, Millie, he told me his dad had him up at daybreak, they prepared your breakfast and lunches for the trip, I'm sure Bastien had eaten before your eyes opened." A sweet smile followed, and he motioned for them to sit and consume the wonderful meal of Eggs Benedict.

"Oh, Jeremiah, thank you for taking care of all of this for us, it's such a relief and I can tell that your dad feels much better about having Bastien travel with us. Are you sure you can spare him?"

He laughed. "If Jean Claude says, yes, then it's a *yes*. You don't want to get me on his bad side, do you?" He chuckled again and tilted his head toward her. "These chefs can be so temperamental."

At that moment Bastien and Robbie Ferguson appeared with three small pieces of luggage, two makeup cases and a parcel of brown paper, tied with string, that the ladies could smell from their table.

Bastien greeted them. “Good morning, Captain, ladies, gentlemen.” He glanced toward Millie. “Are you ready to head to the train station, Mrs. Millie? The water taxi is here and I have a taxi waiting on the pier.”

Millie gave Bastien a hug. “My goodness, you’re efficient.”

Bastien grinned, leaned in and whispered, “I have strict orders from my father to care of your every need. Shall we go?”

George pulled her in. “Love you, Millie,” and gave her a kiss.

She followed with, “I love you too, George,” and cut her eyes toward Jeremiah. “Take care of your dad. He will be lonesome without me,” she grinned, “or at least he’d better be.”

Jeremiah saluted. “Yes, Ma’am, your ladyship!”

Millie noticed Abby giggling in Sam’s ear as they whispered their goodbyes.

Then Bastien led them across the deck and down the gangway.

George, Sam and Jeremiah waited topside as Bastien and the water taxi captain helped the ladies board the small craft. When all were seated, Bastien and the captain shoved the vessel away from the platform, they both stepped to the wheelhouse and the captain pushed the throttle lever. Off they sped. Beautiful Mediterranean blue sea and sky breezed past.

“Abby, doesn’t this scenery remind you of the beautiful color Tony chose for your walls and cabinets?"

"It does, but nothing compares to the real thing." She clamped her hands into fists under her chin. "Just imagine, we'll be cruising through scenery like this for a year!"

"Well, you and your handsome doctor will, but George and I will probably go home after the trial or after the three-month cruise, he's leaving the decision to me."

"Oh Millie, you have to stay at least for the three months. I'd miss you tremendously if you left sooner than that."

"We'll see, Abby. You might want to be rid of me so you can have more honeymoon time with Sam."

She thought for a moment. "Well, we can spend the daytime hours together and reserve the nights for romance," she giggled.

The taxi pulled up to the pier and Bastien leapt to the dock to offer a hand to the ladies as the captain helped them carefully step over the rail, a waiting taxi driver opened the trunk of his new Mercedes, Bastien placed all the bags in, in an orderly manner, while the driver opened the rear door for Millie and Abby. When the trunk was closed, Bastien scrambled into the front passenger seat, the driver hopped in behind the steering wheel, clicked his seatbelt and off they roared.

Chapter 9

At the Train Station

Millie and Abby waited on the platform while a ticket agent checked Bastien in, then the lad escorted them to the train. "Ladies, we have found great favor today. The rear car, the observation lounge, has been reserved strictly for us. No other passengers are allowed in that area today, so you will be able to enjoy the scenery without being bothered by people trying to sell you trinkets or trying to trick you into following their leadership rather than mine."

Abby's mouth flew open. "Millie, do you think, Jeremiah, Sam or George arranged this?"

Millie smiled. "Perhaps all three, dear."

Bastien beamed. "Ladies, may I suggest you take seats on the ocean-side of the train carriage, facing forward, for the best view."

Abby tipped her head. "Thank you, Bastien, your advice sounds brilliant."

Just as they were seated, the train began to ease forward, the station crept past slowly, then the train began to gain speed.

Millie glanced at her sister. "My goodness, this is smooth and quiet."

Abby nodded. “I agree, dear, no rumbling and jostling like the old trains back home.”

From across the aisle, Bastien added, “Yes, ladies, this is the Bullet Train, designed and built in France. Its top speed is over two-hundred miles per hour. Once it builds to the desired speed, the wheels fold underneath and the train is propelled magnetically above the rails.”[i]

Throwing her hands to her face, Abby gasped. “Is that safe?”

“Oh yes, madam, quite safe. Its own record speaks for the safety of the train.”

They sat in silence for a few minutes enjoying the scenery as it sped rapidly past.

Bastien stood and addressed them. “Now if you will excuse me,” he placed the parcel of delightful smelling lunch on the table in front of them, “I will go to gather something for you to drink with your lunch.” He bowed slightly and walked away to the front of the car and disappeared through the door.

Seconds later, Abby poked her sister. “Millie, the scenery appears less blurry. Are we slowing down?”

Millie lifted the parcel of food to her nose and sniffed. “Perhaps your vision is adjusting to the speed and,” she propelled the package toward her sister, “smell this food, Abby.”

“Ooo, you’re right it does smell yummy,” but when she faced the window again, she exclaimed, “Millie, we *are* slowing down! Look!”

“We can’t be there yet!” facing the window, “but you’re right Abby! So much for this fancy-dancy train. Has it broken down?”

At that moment the wheels lowered and contacted the track with a jolt.

Abby grabbed the armrest of her seat. “Wow! That was rough.”

The train ground to a halt.

“Let me see if I can tell what’s happening.” Millie pushed up from her seat and walked toward the door where she froze in her tracks.

“What’s wrong, dear?”

“Abby, you’re not going to believe this.” Through the window the rest of the train disappeared from her view, into the distance. She returned to her seat in a daze and plonked down.”

“What is it, Millie?”

“The train’s gone. We’re here alone.”

Abby rose, pushed past her sister and strode toward the door. “Don’t be ridiculous.” Her hands flew up and slammed against the window. “What?” She turned sharply, with eyes bugged wide, then staggered back to her seat.

Clutching their food packet to her chest, Millie stared at her sister, but without warning, she leapt to her feet, grabbed Abby’s wrist and screamed, “Run!” She dashed to the door and shoved it open, hauling her bewildered sister behind her. Racing down the steps and away from the train car, the two charged toward a horse munching on a large pile of fresh hay. Their sudden and erratic approach spooked the animal and it bolted, only seconds before the train car exploded behind them.

Millie and Abby were hoisted off their feet, tumbled through the air and propelled over the pasture fence, landing head-down on the haystack. Millie took a moment to recover her wits, then pushed her legs to the right and landed in a sitting position, as if lounging in a recliner.

Abby followed suit in a clockwise fashion, clonking Millie on the head with her feet, as she too ended up in a reclining situation.

"Oh Abigail! For goodness sake!"

At that instant, a swathe of hay cascaded from above, covering them head to toe.

"I'm sorry, Millie, I didn't mean …"

Millie grabbed her sister's arm. "Shhhh!"

The sound of a car engine zoomed into the area, men's voices drew their attention. Both sat motionless, but strained to see through the rough veil of straw.

Three men encircled the demolished train parts. Foreign-sounding syllables drifted into the hay.

Abby whispered. "They must be speaking Darija, Sam told me about it."

Millie tugged her arm. "Shhh!" again was the reply.

The men pushed around parts of seats, walls, flooring and other debris, flailing their arms.

One of the men shouted something and scanned the horizon. He faced the haystack and Millie could see an eyepatch covering his left eye, the half-moon-shaped black leather, glinted in the sun. He squinted his right eye, but apparently saw nothing and turned to the others, shouting a command.

The three returned to their Jeep on the far side of the wreckage, made a U-turn and peeled-off in the direction of Tangier.

Millie exhaled a long low breath. "Abigail, I don't think this was an accident! I think those men were searching for our bodies in the wreckage. Thanks to your clumsy legs and feet, the Lord covered us with this straw to shield us from their view." She knew her sister well enough to believe that Abby grinned beneath the straw.

"Thank you, Millie."

Then in Abby's voice Millie sensed a frown.

"I think."

Millie realized she still clutched the lunch pouch with one hand and Abby's arm with the other and chuckled. "I think we're safe to dust off a little straw."

Turning loose of her sister, she and Abby swished their arms to free their upper torsos from the scratchy hay.

Millie smiled at Abby. "Since we're seated and it's lunchtime, perhaps we should take a moment to dine."

Abby stared at her sister. "My goodness, Millie, after an explosion, you can still eat?"

Millie chuckled, but then sounded more serious. "It might be a long walk back to Tangier, we need our strength and there's no use letting this food go to waste." She opened the wrapped package and two luscious-looking folded sandwiches sat side-by-side with two small, clear containers of exotic salad perched atop each. "Now if we only had something to drink."

The straw rustled and Abby produced two pouches of water, one from each pocket of her linen jacket. "Will these do?" She beamed. "Sam shoved them into my pockets as we were saying goodbye."

"That wonderful man! Yes, those will be excellent." Reaching for one of the pouches, Millie ripped the foil closure across the top and squirted some of the liquid into her mouth. "Ahhh, I needed that." She thrust some food toward her sister. "Here dear, here's your salad and sandwich. Now if we only had forks."

Abby laughed. "Look on top of your sandwich."

Neatly wrapped forks and napkins lay encased in clear plastic between the main course and the salad. "Oh my, I'm going to have to give Jean Claude a big hug for this." She glanced at her sister. "Let's pray," they gripped hands and Millie continued. "Heavenly Father, thank you for telling me to run before the explosion and for lifting us with your mighty hands and placing us in this haystack. And thank you for using Abby to cause the cascade of straw to cover us. Your love and protection are beyond measure. Please bless this food and bless Jean Claude for gifting us with such a scrumptious meal and protect Bastien, in Jesus' name, amen."

Ooos, ahhs and some smacking accompanied the devouring of the delightful lunch, after which Millie stood and brushed the straw from her hair and clothing. "Now for a restroom break." She looked around, but flat land and low, stubbly grass lay as far as the eye could see.

Abby stood and dusted herself. "I have an idea." She scooped several arms-full of straw, then scrapping and scrunching, produced a low wall of hay. She stood and looked around. "I don't see anyone, so here goes." The prim, proper lady squatted in the middle of the ring of horse food. "Do you have any tissue, Millie?

A hand holding a facial tissue jutted over the privacy wall.

"Thank you, dear." Abby stood and straightened her clothes. "Next!"

Millie laughed, but pushed aside some hay for a clean place to stand. "I must admit, this is quite remarkable, for two city girls, that is."

When Millie finished, Abby appeared with a scrap of metal from the train wreckage, moved the clean straw back to the haystack and scraped dust over anything that should not be seen or discussed. "There! Now the horse has his clean hay back and all traces of the unsightly are … un-sight-able." She grinned.

"You are a true marvel, Abigail. Even in the remotest of places, you manage to be delicate."

A smile spread across her face. "Thank you, Millie!"

But the smile melted from Millie's face. "Which way do you think we should go? We could be a hundred miles from Tangier by now."

Abby glanced up and down the track. "Maybe Bastien came back with our drinks and found that we were missing. I'm sure he would have stopped the train."

Millie nodded in agreement. "If he could have, yes, I'm sure he would have, but who did this? Who were those three men and who is trying to kill us?"

Chapter 10

The Arrangements

Millie turned to her sister. “You know, Abby, I’ve been thinking about who arranged for us to be the only ones in that Observation Car. I’m sure now that it wasn’t George, Sam or Jeremiah. That would be too much of a co-inky-dinky. It had to be those three men who searched the wreckage, or whoever sent them, don’t you agree?”

Abby pulled her lips to one side and nodded. “Yes, I think you’re right. It would have been too much of a coincidence for it to have been anyone in our family, but at least we can rest in the notion that whoever it was, they weren’t willing to blow-up a train car full of people just to get at the two of us.”

Millie stared squarely at her sister. “I’m sure it’s not the two of us they want dead, Abigail, it’s me because I’m going to testify against Ferdinand. You should’ve stayed with Sam where you’d be safe.”

Abby folded her arms and stomped. “But if I hadn’t been with you, who would have clonked you on the head and caused an avalanche of hay?”

A robust laugh followed. “Indeed, sweet Abigail, who else indeed?” She hugged her sister. “So now we need to pray, I don't have a clue what we're supposed to do or which direction to go." They stood facing each other and joined hands, as Millie prayed. "Heavenly Father, thank you again for your protection and provision, now we need to know where to go, what to do and who to trust, in Jesus' name, amen."

As soon as they opened their eyes, an approaching, siren and flashing light caught their attention in the distance.

"What should we do Millie?"

"I think we should hide." Millie shuffled behind the haystack and dropped to her knees on the ground with Abby close on her heels.

Two Moroccan Police cars slid to a stop in the dirt next to the track, dust whooshed up in a cloud and drifted to the east, an official stepped from the lead vehicle.

Two uniformed officers exited the second car.

The first man shouted, "Fouillez la zone."

The officers walked, one on either side of the tracks and scanned the debris.

After walking the length of the wreckage and back, one of the men shouted, "Il n'y a personne icic."

The man in the suit turned and began to walk toward the fence.

Millie pushed closer to Abby at the center of the haystack.

As the man approached, he began to sing. "Notre Dieu est un Dieu impressionnant."

Behind the pile of hay, two pair of wide eyes, turned toward each other.

Millie whispered, "He's singing, 'Our God is an Awesome God,'" and gave a thumbs up sign to her sister. They both rose slowly and stepped from behind the mound of hay.

The gentleman smiled as he faced them. “Es-tu en sécurité, Mesdames.”

Millie took the lead. “Oui, monsieur, Officier, nous sommes des Américains en route pour … Oh, English, s'il vous plait.” They stepped his direction.

He nodded. “English will be fine. My name is Chief Inspector Alif Kadiri.”

Millie extended her hand over the fence. “I am Mildred Williams and this is my sister Abigail Fielding. We were on our way to Marrakesh where I am to testify at an Interpol Tribunal.”

Clutching her hand, he frowned. “Is this the case of the stolen yacht and the injured seamen?”

“Yes, it is. I was the person responsible for turning in the man who deceived the lady and setup the crew of the Amelia Rose. He was acting on behalf of some mercenaries who took control of the vessel. My role in the tribunal is to verify my testimony against him. The authorities hope that my being there and my testimony will pressure him into revealing the name or names of those who hired him to deliver the yacht to them, in exchange for a lighter sentence, of course.”

“I see, madam. It would appear that you are involved in a case far more serious in nature than anyone had realized. Allow me to help you to this side of the fence.” He held two wires apart as wide as possible, as Millie and Abby crawled through.

“Merci beaucoup, Chief Inspector Kadiri.”

He paused for a moment with his finger and thumb encasing his chin. “I have just received my orders. I will escort you personally to Marrakesh and deliver you safely to the Interpol authorities."

"Thank you, monsieur, that would be so kind of you, but how did you receive your orders? You've not been on the radio. Are you wearing an earpiece?"

He lifted one eyebrow and tipped his eyes upward. "In this case, I need no radio, madam." He smiled. "Will you join me and my driver in the lead car?"

While the official instructed the driver of the second car, Millie hooked her arm in Abby's and strolled toward the first vehicle. "It seems we've been sent a guardian angel, Abby. I'm sure we'll be fine from here on out."

Chief Inspector Kadiri returned and opened the rear door of the squad car.

Millie and Abby scooted inside.

He climbed into the front passenger seat and lifted the microphone.

Millie translated. "It seems he is informing headquarters that the train car explosion appears to have been an attempt on the life of a vital American witness in the Interpol Tribunal. He says," she gasped.

Abby leaned toward her and whispered, "What is it, Millie?"

"I think they have dubbed this the Italian Mafioso or La Cosa Nostra Trial." Her eyes flashed toward her sister. "Abigail, it appears that Ferdinand was working for the Italian mafia."

Abby's mouth flew open, and her head whipped toward Millie. "I can't believe he was that bad, Millie. Surely, he didn't know who he was working for."

Millie narrowed her eyes. "Or maybe he had no choice."

The pleasant voice of the Chief Inspector, tinged

with a French accent, drifted over into the back seat. "Ladies, are you sure you are not injured?"

Millie smiled. "We are fine, thank you, but you should know that before you arrived, three men roared up in a Jeep and inspected the wreckage. I suspect they were looking for our bodies."

He glanced over his shoulder. "May I ask how you evaded them?"

Millie made the same sign with her eyes that he had used. "Our *commanding officer* took care of us. It involved being hurled by the explosion into that stack of hay and covered by its top sliding down over us. Then after they left, we indulged in the most delicious lunch which had been supplied to us by the chef of the *Princess of the Med.* His son Bastien had accompanied us on the train."

"Where is this young man now, madam?"

She glanced at Abby. "We're not certain. He had left us alone in the Observation Car to go and get beverages for us."

"You were alone in the car?"

Abby interjected. "Yes, just the two of us, Bastien had told us that the man at the ticket window had told him that we had found great favor and that we had the observation car all to ourselves. We assumed our husbands had arranged it."

"Madam, that is quite impossible, the Observation Lounge is the only car on the train that is open to everyone. Anyone, at any time, could have accessed the car. This is very strange indeed. Who are your husbands whom you thought had such great power?"

Millie leaned forward. "My husband is George Williams, he's part-owner of the *Princess of the Med.*

His son, my stepson, Jeremiah is the Captain." She lifted her hand toward her sister. "Abigail's husband is the Chief Medical Officer of the ship, Dr. Samuel Fielding."

"As impressive as they sound, madam, they do not possess the power nor wealth to secure your privacy in the Lounge on the Bullet Train. This has all the markings of a professional attempt at assassination."

Gasps escaped from both Millie and Abby.

Chapter 11

Marrakesh

Abby turned toward her sister and pressed her palms together. "Oh, Millie, we have to let George and Sam know what's going on."

"No, we can't! They'd be worried sick."

Abby's eyebrows shot up. "And rightly so, don't you think?" She leaned toward the front seat. "Senior!"

Millie twisted her lips. "Oh Abigail! It's monsieur."

"Very well! Monsieur Kadiri, would you be so kind as to have the captain of the *Princess of the Med* notified of our situation. They are on their way through the Strait of Gibraltar, heading toward the port of Tangier Med."

"Indeed, madam." He lifted the mic.

Abby grabbed the back of the seat and said, "But try not to scare him to death, please."

The officer chucked. "Indeed, I will do my best madam." The microphone crackled and French floated smoothly both directions.

Millie folded her arms. "There, are you satisfied? He's asked them to alert Jeremiah that we are safe and in protective custody, but that there had been an incident earlier in the day. They also want to know if

Bastien has returned safely to the ship and he instructed the Tangier police to contact the Interpol Representative in Marrakesh to inform him of the problem."

In response, Abby also folded her arms. "By problem, I assume he means the murderous attempt on your life?"

The Chief Inspector responded. "Yes, madam, that is exactly what I meant. We will not tolerate this terrorism in our country."

Abby sheepishly shrugged her shoulders. "Sorry, Inspector and thank you."

He smiled over the seat at her. "It is a pleasure to be entrusted with the care of such brave and noble ladies. Now, if you will relax, it will take us about three more hours by car to reach Marrakesh. The train is much swifter, but in your case, that form of transportation is no longer recommended. While we travel, would you be so kind as to tell me what you remember about your journey and the three men who searched the wreckage today."

Abigail started. "We were fortunate in having the chef, Jean Claude's son accompany us."

He looked at his notepad and nodded. "Yes, that would be Bastien, correct?"

"Yes, he is a most pleasant young man, he went to the window at the train station and gave our tickets to the agent."

"So, you already had your tickets?"

Millie nodded, "Yes, my stepson Jeremiah had ordered them for us and handed them to Bastien this morning, just before we left."

Kadiri questioned further. "How did you get to the

train station?"

Abby responded, "First by the water taxi that Bastien had requested, it took us from the ship to the pier and he had also called for a taxi and it was waiting there for us."

"What was the name of the cab company?"

Millie cleared her throat and looked at Abby who shrugged. Millie said, "I don't remember seeing a name. The driver opened the door for us."

"Did it have a light on the roof?"

Millie shook her head. "Sorry, I don't remember seeing one."

He placed his elbow on the back of the seat. "What color was the taxi?"

Abby perked up. "I know this answer. it was a black Mercedes."

"Thank you, madam." Then the man's voice took on a strange tone. "Ladies, could either or both of your husbands be after your wealth?"

Millie burst out laughing. "Uhhh, no! George is part owner of the cruise line, like I said earlier, and he owns a mansion. I had moved in with my sister because we were both lonely after losing our husbands, but truthfully, I was having trouble making ends meet after Henry passed away. We have been offered a substantial reward from the various individuals who lost property because of the man I'm to testify against, but it will not be released to us until after the Tribunal has concluded. Trust me when I say," her eyes turned toward the ceiling of the vehicle, "our *commanding officer* has the situation well in hand."

Kadiri placed his hand on his chest. "Forgive my suspicious nature, mesdames, my apologies."

Millie leaned forward and patted his shoulder. "It's perfectly understandable, if you feel you must investigate them, feel free, but all you will find are two formerly unhappy widowers, now married to two formerly unhappy widows, but all four of whom are now very happy."

"Thank you for your graciousness, Mrs. Williams, as you know, I'm only doing my job." He smiled. "Now, when you were at the ticket office, could you hear what Bastien said to the ticket agent?"

Abby glanced at Millie. "Well, no, we were too busy looking around and we knew that Jean Claude had told Bastien to take care of us, so we were being typical tourists, I guess you could say."

The Chief Inspector lifted the handset. "The microphone clicked and mingled with the French and Arabic, were the names Jean Claude and Bastien."

Abby leaned forward. "You don't think they were involved, do you?"

"Merely a formality to run a check on every name that comes up in a case. Please continue."

Millie took the lead again. "Well, when Bastien returned from the ticket window, that's when he told us that we had found great fortune or great favor, I forget which, to have the train car to ourselves today."

His brows bent low over his eyes. "Then what happened?"

Abby picked up the conversation. "We got aboard the train and when it started to move, I commented on how smooth it was, then Bastien explained to us about the Bullet Train and the magnetic technology."

The Chief Inspector rubbed his chin. "So, he was aware of the workings of the Bullet?"

She lifted her hands. “Isn’t everyone? He made it sound normal to know how it worked.”

Kadiri reached for the notepad again in his shirt pocket. “Then what happened, madam.”

Millie interrupted. “Then he placed our meal packet on the table and said that he was going to get drinks for us.”

“So, was that the first you knew of the meal?”

“No, Jeremiah had told us that Jean Claude had gotten Bastien up early and they had prepared breakfast for us and a lunch for our trip. We had smelled it for hours.” She laughed.

Abby added. “The smell was wonderful and the flavor lived up to its aroma.”

Kadiri looked back and smiled. “So even after nearly being blown up, being tossed through the air like dolls, landing in a haystack and watching scoundrels search for your body parts, you ladies had an appetite?”

They heard the driver snicker.

Millie leaned forward and arched her eyebrow. “When you trust the person driving, there’s no need to lose your appetite.”

The driver pressed his lips together, but said nothing.

Kadiri smiled at the driver, then continued. “You two ladies are amazing. I’m not even sure I would have been able to eat after such a harrowing ordeal.”

Millie grinned, leaned forward and patted his shoulder again. “You could have if you’d been smelling that food for hours like we had. Jean Claude is a marvelous chef.”

He laughed. “Okay, so tell me about the three men who searched for you. What do you remember?”

Millie scrunched her eyebrows. "As you know we were shrouded by straw, all I saw were three swarthy-looking men, all about the same size and with dark hair, but one thing that I do remember is that one of them, he seemed to be the leader, wore a half-moon-shaped, black leather eyepatch covering his left eye. It was very distinctive."

Kadiri turned sharply. "Are you certain?"

Millie nodded. "Yes, I'm certain. He paused and looked straight at the hay pile. Oh, and there was something above the eyepatch, but I was too far away to tell you for certain what it was."

The Chief Inspector relaxed some. "Why did you think he was the leader, Mrs. Williams?"

She lifted her palms. "He shouted orders to the other two and they followed them without hesitation."

The driver whispered, "Balthazar."

Chapter 12

Who?

Abby lifted her shoulders and palms. "Who is Balthazar?"

Kadiri gave a strong look to the driver before answering. "According to legend, Mrs. Fielding, Balthazar is a fallen angel who faked his own death and came to earth bringing many destructive weapons with him. He has supposedly lived a hedonistic lifestyle here ever since."

Abby leaned forward. "By here, do you mean Morocco or just here on earth?"

"Well, specifically, the Mediterranean area; Italy, Greece, northern Africa, including Morocco and Egypt. Until a few years ago, people in law enforcement considered him a myth or legend. Now we suspect that someone has adopted the persona and is conducting criminal activities under that name. Until recently, he had been as elusive as a specter, giving credence to the myth."

Millie echoed. "Until recently! What changed?"

"I hate to say this, but he has been leaving a trail of bodies. Prior to the last couple of years, there were thefts and brazen midnight robberies, but no deaths or physical assaults, but now, the pattern includes a rising body-count." He looked over his shoulder. "Thankfully, your *commanding officer* placed his benevolent angels and straw, around you." He smiled, but it faded quickly. "I have mixed emotions about you testifying at this tribunal, on the one hand, we need brave law-abiding citizens to step forward and help us, but again … with this explosion today, I fear that he sees you as a direct threat. That places you in imminent danger, Mrs. Williams. I will liaise with the Interpol Representative and we will compare notes. Do you know his name?"

Millie nodded. "Yes, the man who came to the *Princess of the Sea* in the Caribbean, to escort Ferdinand Modesto to Morocco, was a Brit, named Bryan Saunders."

"Very good, I look forward to meeting Mr. Saunders. Ladies, may I suggest you get some rest before we reach Marrakesh. Even though you seem to be faring well, it has been a stressful day. If you can—please sleep, I will wake you when we reach the city."

Leaning forward, the sound of strain filled Millie's voice. "I just have one request."

"Yes, madam?"

"If these back doors won't open from the inside, please don't leave us alone in the car for any reason."

"Certainly, madam, but may I ask why?"

She blew out a tense breath, "Because of Ferdinand and all of this rigmarole, I was kidnapped and held hostage in the Caribbean. I haven't fancied being locked in anywhere since then."

Kadiri stared over his shoulder. "And yet you are willing to testify. I did not think I could be more surprised, but again, you have amazed me, madam. I certainly will respect your wishes, now try to get some rest, please."

Chapter 13

Zzzzzs

The hum of the motor and the smooth car ride lulled Millie and Abby to sleep. Soft Zzzzs rolled forward from the back seat.

As they approached Marrakesh, the driver smiled at Kadiri and whispered, "Seems a shame to wake them."

A whisper returned from the Chief Inspector. "Yes, it does, but we will respect Mrs. Williams' wishes, I can't even imagine testifying at this tribunal after all that she's suffered. She's an amazing lady."

The car slowed to a stop outside the courthouse where Kadiri had arranged to meet Saunders.

A pale, British-type stood waiting on the steps.

Kadiri whispered instructions to his driver. "Under no circumstances are you to leave these ladies alone. Do not leave this car for a second! Do you understand? And be on guard, in case we were followed."

"Oui, monsieur."

Kadiri stepped from the vehicle and eased the door closed, but the click alerted Millie.

She leaned forward. "Driver, where are we?"

He responded. "We have arrived at the court

building in Marrakesh and Chief Inspector Kadiri is meeting with Monsieur Saunders." He pointed to the two men on the steps. "He instructed me to remain in the car with you and your sister."

At that moment, Abigail stretched. "Are we there yet?"

Millie turned to her sister. "Yes, dear, we're here and Mr. Kadiri is talking with Mr. Saunders, just there." She pointed out the driver's side window.

Abby leaned to the window, knocked and waved. "Yoo-hoo, Bryan."

Millie pulled her arm down. "For goodness sake, Abby. I don't think they would want attention drawn to us."

She placed her fingers on her lips. "Oh, yes, silly me, I should have thought."

Kadiri returned to the car. "Ladies, Mr. Saunders suggested we change your hotel, just in case those who are after you, have advanced information."

Millie bristled. "Well, I can assure you that any *advanced information* did not come from Jeremiah or any of our family!"

He turned to her, placing his arm on the back of the seat and smiled. "And I can also *assure you*, madam that I meant no intentional reflection on your family, but someone had been informed that you would be on that train this morning and which car you would be in, so I think changing your accommodations would be wise. I instructed Mr. Saunders to handle the matter, but I will accompany you and check out the situation."

Millie placed her hand on his arm. "Thank you and I'm sorry I was too quick to conclude that you might still suspect Jeremiah, or one of our husbands."

"Let me just say, Mrs. Williams, that I would never want to 'ruffle your feathers,' as American's might say and that I would always want you to be on my side. You are a fierce defender," and he flashed her a charming smile revealing his pearly white teeth. "Now let's proceed to the hotel Saunders mentioned."

When they arrived, Saunders leaned on the doorpost outside a seedy hotel.

Abby placed her hand on the window. "This doesn't look exactly safe."

"I agree, Mrs. Fielding, but perhaps Saunders felt a low-profile accommodation would be less conspicuous."

Abby leaned back. "Well, I can tell you that our husbands wouldn't be happy with this place."

Millie patted her sister's arm. "I agree, Abigail, but I'm trusting that these gentlemen know their business."

"Well, okay, but if the sheets aren't clean, I'm not staying!"

Millie laughed. "That's a given, dearest, now let's see what this place looks like inside."

The driver stepped out and opened the back door.

Abby swung her legs from the car and Millie slid across the seat. As they exited, Kadiri walked around the rear of the vehicle, glancing up and down the street. He placed his hand on Millie's back. "Ladies, let's get you off the street."

They proceeded to the hotel entrance where Saunders gave-way, allowing the entourage to pass. He glanced down the street, then trailed them into the tiny lobby.

The clerk beamed. "Messieurs and mesdames,

welcome to the Saffron Hotel, your hum away from hum. The genttaman request Englaze and it is moi pleazure to speak unto you in your nateev tonge."

Saunders stepped forward and the grin melted from the clerk's face. "Key, please."

"Oui, monsieur." His hand thrust forward with a dull key and a tag marked 201.

Saunders pointed to the narrow stairs.

Kadiri led the way, followed by Millie, Abby and Saunders in the rear. At the top of the stairs the Chief Inspector paused and peeked around the corner. The short hallway spread before him with two doors on each side. "Saunders, give me the key." They passed it up the line, he reached back to take it. "Mrs. Williams, wait here." He rushed to the first door, unlocked it and swung it open wide. Peering in he scanned the room, stepped out and motioned for Millie to move.

Abby followed close behind and both rushed to the door and darted inside. Abby grabbed the bedspread and flung it back. "Well, the sheets appear to be clean. I guess we can stay."

Saunders stepped in behind them.

Millie glanced around. "Where's the bathroom? It's been a long trip."

Just inside the doorway, Kadiri pointed his thumb over his shoulder. "It must be over here. Let me check it out." He backed across the hall, scanning both directions. The door swung in and banged against the tub.

Abby jumped. "What was that?"

Millie patted her arm. "It was just the door, dear, please try to calm down, Monsieur Kadiri and Mr. Saunders are right here."

"Okay, I'm sorry, I didn't realize how jumpy I am."

Kadiri returned to the room. "That's perfectly understandable, Mrs. Fielding. Now, Mrs. Williams, I've checked the bathroom and it's secure, but as a precaution, will you talk to me while you're in there. I'll wait outside the door."

Millie smiled. "I'll even sing you an aria, if you like." She walked past him.

"That will not be necessary, unless you would enjoy singing." He returned her smile.

She entered the bathroom and closed the door. "Should I lock it or not?"

"Whichever you prefer, I will be right here, but I will respect your privacy unless there is any sign of trouble."

"La-di-da-di-daaaaah," followed by the gush of a flush. Water running from the faucet signaled the finale, the door swung open, Millie's arm flew to the sides, as she announced, "Ta-da!"

Kadiri laughed. "You are remarkable, Mrs. Williams."

"Please call me Millie."

"Very well, if you will call me Alif."

She entered the room. "Done! Now, Abby, do you fancy a trip to the facilities?"

Abby's shoulders were tight, near her ears. "If you will come with me."

Millie placed her hand on Abby's arm. "Monsieur Kadiri, I mean, Alif, will be right outside the door and there isn't enough room for two people in there, unless one of us stands in the tub." She grinned at her sister.

"Well, okay, then," Abby paused, "you can stand in the tub." A roar of laughter from Millie caused

Saunders to jump.

He chuckled. “My goodness, even I’m jumpy.”

Abby crossed to the restroom while Alif stood guard at the door.

When she returned to the room, he followed her in. “Saunders, can you wait here with the ladies while I arrange guards and transportation for them for the duration of the tribunal. When do you need Mrs. Williams at the courthouse?”

“I can do some prep here at the room now, but she will be needed in court in the morning.”

The Chief Inspector nodded. “Bon, I will make the arrangements with the local officials, but I will need to return to my office in Tangier, then come back in the morning. Can you stay with them through the night?”

“Yes, I will place a chair next to the door in the hall.”

Alif turned to Millie and Abby. “Very well, ladies, I leave you in the capable hands of Mr. Saunders.”

Millie extended her hand. “Thank you, Alif, I’m sure we will be fine and thank you for coming to our rescue earlier today.”

He shook her hand, placed his left hand atop hers, then bowed slightly. “It was my pleasure, Millie. Au revoir,” then turned to Bryan. “Until tomorrow, Saunders, I leave you to it, I’m sure there is no need to explain the gravity of this situation to you.”

“No need at all, monsieur. I will take the greatest of care of my star witness and her sister.”

Alif opened the door, scanned the hall and moved out, closing the door behind him.

“Ladies, we should settle in and begin to prepare for

tomorrow. Mrs. Williams, will you join me at the table?"

Chapter 14

Prep Begins

After a couple of hours of discussion Millie stretched. "I'm getting stiff, maybe the explosion did more to my body than I realized. I think I need to get up and move around."

Saunders pulled back the curtain to survey the street below. "Perhaps you would like a short walk in the market. I think that would be safe."

Abby looked up from her catnap. "I don't think that would be wise."

Looking through the window again, Saunders nodded. "It looks like a typical night at the market. I'm sure it will be okay."

Millie stood and pulled her shoulders back. "That would be great, besides we need to pick up some clothes for court tomorrow. All of our luggage blew-up with the observation lounge car," she gasped, "and you know, it never crossed my mind that our purses, with our passports were destroyed too."

Abby laughed and reached under her shirt to pull out a fanny pack. "Well, while you weren't looking, I put both of our passports and driver's licenses in here for safe keeping."

Wide eyes and a smile greeted her. "What made you

do that, not that I'm not grateful."

"I was concerned about what Jeremiah said about pickpockets," she tipped her head toward her sister, "and you aren't very careful with your purse, Millie."

Millie's shoulders arched back. "I am too!"

Abby grinned. "Did you know that I had removed your passport and ID?"

Slouched shoulders accompanied her reply. "Okay, you made your point. It seems you were being prompted by the Lord, Abigail. Good for you for listening and obeying."

A satisfied smile greeted Millie, then a momentary pause. "You are being serious, aren't you?"

With a chuckle and a smile, she said, "Yes, dearest, I'm being serious." She turned to their keeper. "Mr. Saunders, shall we go shopping?"

"This way ladies."

They followed him down the stairs, to the front door. There, Saunders leaned toward the street and looked both ways. "I think we're clear. Follow me closely, please."

An aroma greeted their noses.

Abby gave a long sniff. "What is that wonderful smell?"

Saunders pulled in a deep breath. "I believe what you are smelling is the famous Marrakesh Snail Soup."

Abby's lips twisted. "Yuck!"

He laughed. "No, no, it is a delicacy here and I insist you try it. The snails are chocolate brown and protrude slightly from their shells when cooked, you fish them out with a long, thin skewer to eat them. The flavorsome broth is reported to have restorative and digestive health properties. For those reasons, if no other, I insist you and Mrs. Williams try the soup."[ii]

They approached a stall.

Millie took in a deep breath. "Well, if smells delicious, Abby, if you just forget what you're eating, I'm sure that will help," and she smiled.

Saunders ordered three bowls. When each was placed on the outer edge of the stall, he handed one to Millie, one to Abby and took one for himself. "Bon appetite, Mesdames."

With a chuckle, Millie sipped the broth from the serving dish. "My goodness that is flavorful and spicy, I would never have guessed. It almost resembles soy sauce, but not salty and quite good. Give it a whirl, Abby."

Abby's nose scrunched.

Millie tapped her sister with her elbow. "Really dear, give it a try."

She lifted the dish to her lips with a look on her face, as if facing a hangman's noose. "Okay, but … ." Tipping the bowl, a tiny amount passed over her lips. "Oh, my goodness! It's delicious."

Grabbing the skewer from her serving dish, Millie placed her bowl on the rail again and picked up a snail. "Let's see what these little rascals are like." With the skewer, she plucked one from its shell, tilted her head back and plopped one into her mouth. As she chewed she said, "What a surprise. They're tender and delicious, not at all like the chewier American variety I've tried before. Give in and try it, Abs."

"Do I have to pick it up with my hands?"

"Oh, Abby." Using her skewer, Millie plucked one of Abby's snails from its shell and dangled it before her. "Now, eat this."

Abby's lips puckered in disgust, but she obediently opened her mouth and closed her eyes.

Millie pushed the snail in.

Forced to chew, Abby's eyes sprang open. "I can't believe how good that is. It's not slimy at all."

Saunders laughed. "But I would *not* recommend eating them raw.

Abby gagged but recovered. "Bryan, that was disgusting."

He chuckled. "Sorry, Mrs. Fielding." He pushed cups of fresh squeezed orange juice at them. "Nothing disgusting in these, I promise."

Abby took a sip. "This is a wonderful complement to the," she frowned, "the … soup," then she smiled.

Following their respite, they walked on to the first stall with clothes, Millie spotted a skirt. "Let me see if this will fit."

Saunders rested his hand on Abby's shoulder. "Mrs. Fielding, will you stay close to your sister?" He pointed across the small street. "I'm going to check things out over there."

Abby stepped in behind her sister.

Millie approached the merchant to discuss a blouse to go with the skirt, Abby stayed at her side, as directed. Not being able to communicate her wishes, she looked for Saunders. He was talking to someone on the other side of the street. "Yoo-hoo, Mr. Saunders."

His chin dropped, his eyes widened and he rushed to her. "Yes, is there a problem?"

"It seems this man is unable to understand my request for a top to go with this," and she held up the skirt.

In broken Darija, he addressed the seller, who produced a suitable top, but far too small.

Millie held the shirt against her body and the man nodded, producing a more reasonable fit.

Saunders brokered the exchange and paid the man from his own pocket.

"Thank you, Saunders, I'll see that you are reimbursed."

"No need, madam. I will file it under expenses. After all, you have come here at great risk and at great loss of property. I'm sure Interpol can spare a few Moroccan dirham to assist you." He backed away.

Millie picked up the skirt and blouse to carry, but the merchant handed her a straw bag. She waved him off, but he persisted.

Abby tugged at her sleeve. "It might be considered rude to refuse the bag."

Millie nodded and accepted the gift, placing her garments inside. As she turned to walk away the man started shouting indecipherable words. She stopped and stared his direction. Two men ran to Millie and grabbed her arms.

Abby started shouting, "Millie, what's going on?"

Held tightly by the two men, Millie shouted, "Where's Saunders, Abby? Can you see him?"

Abby looked around, but Saunders was nowhere in sight.

A police officer came to the scene and talked with the vendor. Neither she nor Abby could understand a word, but the policeman took out handcuffs, took the bag from her and pulled Millie's hands behind her back.

As the officer turned Millie around, she saw the man with the black leather, half-moon eyepatch grinning at her. "Abigail, it's the leader of the men who searched the train."

About that time, Saunders appeared. "What's going on?"

Millie yelled at him, "Perhaps you can tell us. That man shoved a straw bag at me and insisted, so I took it, then he started shouting, that's when all heck broke loose. Where were you?"

"I was chasing a pickpocket that lifted my wallet. I'm sorry I left you alone."

She twisted her wrists. "Saunders show this officer your credentials and get me out of these handcuffs!"

"I'm afraid I can't, the thief got away."

Abby stomped her foot. "Then tell this copper to take the man and his cashbox with us to the station."

Again, undecipherable words exchanged, but the policeman took the money box and tucked it under his arm, much to the merchant's surprise and demanded that he follow them to the station.

Chapter 15

The Police Station

A large arched doorway, topped by a stained-glass window, ushered them into an entryway tiled with pale amber flooring and edged with a medium blue border. A darker amber wall guided them into a large room of what appeared to be a police station.

Seated behind a wooden counter, a policeman stood to receive the mass of people. Everyone speaking at once caused him to raise his hand abruptly.

Silence followed.

He addressed the younger officer who explained why they were there, then the desk sergeant lifted his phone and requested a Senior Sergeant who spoke English to join him.

A lean, attractive man came to the front desk and nodded to Millie and Abby. "Allow me to introduce myself, I am Senior Sergeant Jaouhari, I will investigate this matter." In his native language he requested that the handcuffs be removed from Mrs. Williams and extra chairs be brought.

The cuffs were immediately removed from Millie's wrists and she rubbed them.

"This way please," he led them into his office, when the chairs arrived, he motioned. "Please be seated." He spoke first to the young officer. When the situation had been explained, the young man was dismissed.

Jaouhari addressed the merchant. After hearing the storekeeper's side of the story, the Senior Sergeant turned to Millie and Abby. "Mesdames, can you tell me your impression of what happened in the market this evening?"

Millie started with the part about the skirt. "Then I had to call, Mr. Saunders to come help me to get an appropriate-sized blouse. You will see the items in the woven bag, there."

The officer pulled the items from the bag. "Mrs. Williams, the merchant says that you purchased these items, then demanded the straw bag and walked away without paying for it."

Abby's feet hit the floor with a thump. "That's a lie! That man," she pointed at the seller.

The storekeeper's eyes popped open wide.

Abby shouted, "He pushed the bag at her."

Millie laid her hand on Abby's arm and admonished her sister. "Abigail, please calm down, this officer, will get to the bottom of the matter."

Abby lowered herself onto her chair. "Forgive me, monsieur. It has been a trying day, with the explosion and all."

His eyes brightened and he leaned back. "Explosion, Madame?"

Abby straightened and pulled her shoulders back. "Yes, we were in the Bullet Train Observation Car that exploded this morning. Of course, we escaped only moments before it blew-up or we wouldn't be here now, in this pickle."

The officer stared back and forth from Abby to

Millie. "One of you is the American who will be testifying at the Interpol Tribunal? Chief Inspector Kadiri told us of your presence here in the city."

Millie tipped her head. "Yes, that is me, monsieur."

Jaouhari leaned his elbows on his desk. "How then have you run the risk of being in the market?"

Millie sighed. "All of my belongings that I brought with me were destroyed in the blast and I needed something clean to wear to court tomorrow."

"Then why steal a straw bag, la dame?"

Abby bristled again. "She did *not* steal anything! That man," she pointed again at the seller, "tried to force the bag on my sister, even after she refused it, but I thought perhaps it might be considered an offense if she refused, so I encouraged her to accept it, but what neither of them knew was that while he was busy, I slipped a coin into his cashbox to cover the cost."

"What type of coin, an American coin, Madame?"

"No, but if you look in the box, monsieur, you will find one of your local coins that it has a smudge of red paint on it. My husband filled my pockets with local money this morning before we left and I found that one annoying since it wasn't clean and shiny."

The officer opened the cashbox and dug through the jumbled coins until he found the one with the smudge of paint and held it up.

Abigail tilted her head and appointed. "You see! And if you dust it for fingerprints, you will find my prints on that coin, monsieur."

Jaouhari smiled. "That will not be necessary, Madame. I thank you for your account of the events and allow me to return the coin to you, it is of far greater value than the cost of the straw bag." He turned to the merchant and a fierce, one-sided monologue took place before he sent the man out of the room, then he turned to Saunders. "And you, monsieur, you should never have left the side of these ladies."

He twisted his hands in his lap. "I know, I apologize to you and to them. A pickpocket stole my wallet and I chased after him, but failed to catch him, now there is a thief in Marrakesh carrying my Interpol identification."

The officer nodded. "I can see your reason for concern, but until Monsieur Kadiri gives us other orders, we will have two men accompany you."

He turned to Millie. "Mrs. Williams, I am so sorry for the inconvenience, please accept our apology and know that every effort will be made to make your visit to our city a safe one from this point forward. We are grateful for your bravery in giving testimony at this tribunal, my brother-by-law was one of the sailors set adrift that day and he suffered extreme dehydration, as a result of the event, he has had heart problems to this day."

Millie leaned on the edge of his desk, her eyes filled with sympathy. "I'm sorry for your brother-in-law's injury and I thank you, monsieur for your kindness in solving this problem. Now if you would, I have a message for Chief Inspector Kadiri."

"Yes, s'il vous plait, what is the message?"

Millie paused, then shook her head. "Never mind, he said he would be back in the morning and since you're sending men to accompany us, it can wait until then, but please inform him of this incident."

"Oui, m'dame." He tipped his head.

Millie extended her hand. "And may I ask what will happen to the merchant?"

Jaouhari shook her hand delicately. "His name will be placed on a list to compare to future complaints. I assure you, he will feel the repercussions, if this was more than a tragic misunderstanding, now, I will have a car and driver return you to your hotel, which is … ?"

"Thank you, Senior Sergeant. We are at the Saffron Hotel."

His eyes flashed open wide. "Mon Dieu! That is one of the least desirable hotels in Marrakesh." His eyes darted to Saunders. "Monsieur, what is the meaning of this? We must move these ladies to a more suitable spot, one safer and closer to the court building, as well."

Saunders head tipped forward and no eye-contact was made. "As you see fit, Senior Sergeant."

Over his office phone, much rattling of the national language took place and moments later an officer appeared at the door and swished his hand. "Pleaz, to follow me."

Millie stood. "Thank you again, Senior Sergeant Jaouhari and please inform Chief Inspector Kadiri of our new location."

He stood and nodded. "Count it as done, Madame."

Millie, Abby and Saunders followed the officer to a waiting car. Once they pulled away from the curb, Saunders spoke. "Ladies, I apologize for all of the troubles. I was caught unaware by the pickpocket today. I should never have chased after him."

Millie's tone was less than forgiving. "So, you said, at the police station."

Abby swatted her arm and mouthed the words. *Millie, be nice.*

She turned to him again. "I'm sorry, Saunders, I'm just tired I suppose. It's late and it's been a difficult day."

They arrived at a hotel near the courthouse. White columns flanked the outer edges of marble stairs, quite a contrast to the dull surroundings of the Saffron Hotel. Upon entering through the tall double doors, smooth mosaic tile led the way to the Registration Desk. Small palm plants stood guard, strategically placed at each outside point of every Moravian Star in the border pattern. The sergeant escorting them approached the desk and introduced himself.

The clerk presented two parcels. "Welcome, Mesdames, to the Marriott Hotel. I understand your luggage and personal items were lost by the train staff, so we have provided you with some necessities to make your stay more pleasant. If there is more that we can do, please do not hesitate to contact the front desk."

Millie smiled. "If two sandwiches could be sent up to our room, it would be most welcomed. The only thing we've eaten since lunch today were two small bowls of your delicious Snail Soup."

He bowed slightly. "I will see to it personally," and pushed a key across the desk to the policeman. "One of our finest rooms for, Mesdames."

Tears rolled down Millie's cheeks. "Thank you, Monsieur, I had not realized how trying this day had been, until your kindness broke through the protective shield which I'd been carrying."

Abby stroked her sister's arm. "Oh, honey, I'm so sorry, you always seem so strong, I'd forgotten how tender your heart really is. Come on, let's get you to the room." She hooked her arm into Millie's bent elbow.

Their escorting officer took the key and led the way to the elevator. The door opened and he swept his hand to indicate, *ladies first.* He followed Millie and Abby while Saunders lagged behind, bringing up the rear.

At the third floor, the door opened again. Saunders stepped out to scan the hallway, but it was not necessary.

Two armed police officers flanked their doorway. The sergeant greeted them and unlocked the door, entered and stepped across the room to check the windows, then opened the door to check their private bath. "All is secure, Mesdames. I wish you a most pleasant night's sleep."

Saunders started to say something, but Millie interrupted. "Thank you, Bryan, I'm sure you will understand if we call it a night, I'm exhausted. Perhaps you can let the officers outside know where you will be staying." A knock at the door silenced her.

The sergeant opened the door an inch, to peek out. The desk clerk's cheerful voice broke the tension. "Sandwiches, salads and soft drinks for the ladies."

He pushed past and rolled a cart to the table where he placed two drinking glasses, silverware, canned sodas and the food, then placed a vase holding a rosebud in the center.

Abby reached in her sweater pocket to pull out two coins and said, "Thank you, Monsieur."

He waved his hand. "No, no, this has already been settled." He backed out and pulled the cart into the hallway.

The sergeant lifted his hand toward the open door. "Saunders, shall we give these ladies some privacy?"

Saunders hesitated, but said with a tip of his head,

"Good evening, ladies," then stepped into the hall, followed by the sergeant, who closed the door behind him.

Millie grabbed her sister by the arm and pulled her close. "Abby, there's something … " But she stopped. "Never mind, dear, perhaps I'm just overly tired, let's eat then get some sleep."

They seated themselves in the chairs abreast the small table.

The top of a soda can popped, Abby poured cola into her glass and took a drink, then a bite of her sandwich. "Well, this isn't as yummy as Jean Claude's folded sandwich, but it is very satisfying."

Another soda can popped-open with a crisp, metallic sound. Soda fizzed as it was poured into a glass. Millie smiled. "I know dear, but this is only a five-star hotel, what can one expect?" Followed by her boisterous laughter filling the room.

Chapter 16

During the Night

Abby was roused from sleep by the sound of a thud and lifted her head.

Millie was being dragged to the door by two men.

Abby tried to stand, but flopped back onto the bed, her body beyond her control. A pale, thin whisper escaped her mouth. “Help, somebody help.”

The hall clock chimed, two.

Chapter 17

A Noise Outside

Abby awoke again to heavy thuds of a fist on their door, then a man's voice, yelling.

Monsieur Kadiri's voice rang out. "Mrs. Williams, Mrs. Fielding are you all right? Open the door, please." The doorknob jiggled.

She struggled to her feet and staggered across the room. Holding onto the adjacent table she unlocked the door.

When it opened, Monsieur Kadiri, burst in. "Are you okay, Mrs. Fielding? Where is Mrs. Williams?"

Tears rolled down Abby's cheeks as she stumbled back onto the bed. "I don't know. Some men took her."

"Why didn't you call out?"

"I tried, but I must have been drugged," and she pointed to the table. "I awoke to a noise and I saw two men dragging Millie to the door. Why didn't the officers outside stop them?"

Kadiri knelt beside her. "They too were drugged, madam. We found them unconscious in the hall with empty cups next to them. They still aren't able to speak." He stood and strode to the table. "I see that one of you did not finish your meal. May I assume that was you, Mrs. Fielding?"

"Yes, I was too tired to finish my sandwich or the drink, but I ate all of my salad. Millie finished hers, then we brushed our teeth and went to bed."

"Where did you get the toothbrushes and night wear?"

"Senior Sergeant Jaouhari must have ordered them. A bundle was waiting for us when we arrived, but Millie asked for the food at the desk when we checked in."

Kadiri patted her hand. "Are you strong enough to get dressed and accompany me to the local station? I need to have a word with Jaouhari and where is Saunders?"

"I'm not sure where he stayed. Senior Sergeant Jaouhari insisted we be moved to this hotel, near the courthouse and he made the arrangements. After we got to the room though, Millie pretty much threw Saunders out. She was very rude, which is not like her, she said she was just tired, but I thought she was still angry with him about the mishap at the market."

"Please, madam, dress as quickly as you can please." Kadiri stepped into the hall, pulling the door, but left it slightly ajar.

Abby struggled into her clothes that she had worn the day before and came out. She appeared slightly disheveled. Kadiri ushered her and his driver into the elevator. As they exited on the ground floor, Saunders strolled through the front door of the hotel, hands in his pockets—whistling. "Good morning, Mrs. Fielding, Monsieur Kadiri. Is Mrs. Williams ready to go to court?"

As they moved closer, the smile washed from his face. He pulled his hands from his pockets. "What's wrong?"

Abby wiped tears from her face as Kadiri answered. "Mrs. Williams has been kidnapped, again, because of this trial. You, sir and Interpol should have made better arrangements for Mrs. Williams. I have already been informed of the debacle on the street last evening."

Saunders' eyebrows knit close together. "Well, it doesn't seem that your local constabulary have done any better."

Kadiri's hands wadded into fists, but remained at his sides. "If I had been in charge, I assure you, Monsieur Saunders, I would have had the Gendarmerie activated. This has been handled in a manner much too lax for the gravity of the situation. I will report all of this to the top Interpol Officials, but in the meantime, we must begin a search for Mrs. Williams."

On the way to the station, Kadiri radioed the day shift to alert Senior Sergeant Jaouhari of the situation.

Moments after they arrived, Jaouhari rushed in. "Monsieur Kadiri, I have had the driver who escorted Mrs. Williams and Mrs. Fielding to the hotel called in, he will be here shortly. I have also gotten the address for the night clerk at the Marriott and have sent men to his home to bring him into the station and local day officers are looking at camera footage for overnight traffic. If we knew the approximate time the abduction happened, things would move much more quickly."

Abby gasped. "It was two A.M. I remember hearing a clock chiming two, oh, why didn't I remember that sooner?"

As they walked to Jaouhari's office, Kadiri placed his hand on her shoulder. "Excellent work, Mrs.

Fielding, now is the perfect time to remember."

In his office, Jaouhari picked up a phone, when the officer answered he instructed the men to check all cameras around the hotel for slightly before two A.M. and after, then he replaced the receiver. "That should hasten our search."

A tap at the door, a man entered. "Sir, the night clerk from the hotel has disappeared. He did not arrive home last night after his shift ended and no one knows where he is."

Jaouhari turned to Kadiri, "It would seem that we now know who drugged the ladies and my officers."

Abby shook her head. "But he seemed so nice, maybe he had no choice."

Kadiri leaned toward her and took her hand. "One always has a choice, Mrs. Fielding."

The door flew open and Sam rushed in. "Abigail, my darling, are you alright?"

She jumped to her feet and flung herself into his arms. Over his shoulder she spotted George, close on his heels.

George entered, firing off questions. "Sergeant, has there been any word? What's being done?"

The phone rang, Jaouhari held up one finger and answered. "Yes, yes, I see, have someone follow that vehicle on the footage, put out a description to all officers and have someone scan the footage near the time the night clerk's shift ended. Report anything suspicious." He hung-up the phone and scanned the faces before him. "Mrs. Fielding … gentlemen, a van was spotted on the camera footage behind the Marriot Hotel. Mrs. Williams, apparently unconscious, was being placed in the back. There was no apparent sign of injury to her."

George blew out a long breath. "I'm glad of that, but it still doesn't ease my mind."

The phone rang again, Jaouhari answered. "Yes," he nodded to the group and continued the conversation aloud, "the night clerk was picked up by a new, black Mercedes, not a taxi? Does it appear that he went willingly? I see, yes, trail it on the footage and put out an alert to stop every new, black Mercedes sighted and give a description of the clerk and the man with the eyepatch."

Abby twisted herself free from Sam's arms and leaned onto Jaouhari's desk. "*New* Mercedes, does that make a difference?"

"Yes, most of Marrakesh's taxis are older Mercedes. The new ones are too expensive for most cabmen. Why do you ask?"

The taxi that took us from the pier to the train station was a *new* black Mercedes. Monsieur Kadiri had asked us if we knew the name of the cab company, but neither of us could recall a name or logo. It didn't occur to me to specify that it was a new car."

Kadiri stood, leaned forward and propped his fists on Jaouhari's desk alongside Abby's hands. "That makes a lot of sense. We need to look for ownership information on all new, black Mercedes in Morocco. And did the clerk go willingly, Jaouhari?"

The Senior Sergeant shook his head. "No, it seems that the young man was a very unwilling participant. He was forced into the car by a man with an eyepatch."

A long, breathy whisper escaped from Abby's lips. "Balthazar."

She shivered and Sam wrapped his arms around her.

Jaouhari picked up the receiver again. “Get me records on every owner of new, black Mercedes in Morocco.” He pushed the receiver back into its cradle. “We have a lot of information already, but now we wait.” He smiled as the phone rang again and scanned the faces before him as he answered. After he hung up, he turned to one person. “The van went to the area of the Saffron Hotel. Can you explain that, Mr. Saunders?”

His eyebrows shot up, his shoulders rose and his palms turned up. “I have no idea, it must be a coincidence.”

Kadiri pushed away from the desk and paced the back of the room. “I don’t like coincidences. Jaouhari, let’s get some plainclothes officers to scour the area of the Saffron. They also need to question any contacts they have in the market.”

George stood and faced him. “I want to go there.”

Jaouhari interrupted. “That may not be a wise idea, Mr. Williams. You’d stand out.”

George wheeled around. “So, a tourist would stand out? I think it would be perfectly natural.”

Kadiri strode toward George. “We will go together, Mr. Williams, it will be as if I’m giving you a tour.” He faced Jaouhari. “Will that be satisfactory with you, Senior Sergeant?”

Jaouhari nodded and motioned through the glass for the desk officer to enter. “Please take Mr. and Mrs. Fielding to a more comfortable place in the station. Have junior personnel see to their every need and keep them informed as you receive news. And,” he stared at Saunders, “Mr. Saunders will wait with them.”

Minutes later, Kadiri, Jaouhari, George and two officers were dropped off within walking distance of the market where Millie had had the altercation with the merchant, the Saffron Hotel lay in the distance just beyond. The two officers flanked George as they walked.

Jaouhari spoke first. “Gentlemen, the shopkeeper who falsely accused Mrs. Williams will recognize me, so I will drift away from you, but if you have any trouble, I will have men close-by.”

Kadiri clapped his hand on George’s back. “We will be fine I’m sure, but please inform us of any reports.”

Jaouhari nodded and crossed the narrow, cobbled street.

George asked, “What was Millie doing in this part of town, it doesn’t exactly look safe for ladies?”

Kadiri’s lips wrinkled. “Following the train car explosion, Saunders had arranged it under the guise of it being a low-profile accommodation. I’m not sure if Jaouhari suspects that he is part of this or that he simply finds him incompetent, either way, I’m sure that is why he was left behind at the station.”

George nodded. “I see, but Bryan Saunders seemed so nice and so, well, competent, when he picked up Ferdinand Modesto in the Caribbean, but can you put in a request for some kind of further background check on him?”

Kadiri lifted his chin. “I’d be surprised if Jaouhari hasn’t already started that process. He seems like a fine officer. I was impressed with his forethought once he was told of the situation. Initially he was placed in charge of your wife’s case because of his excellent English skills, but I see now that God was in control of that as well. May I pray with you Mr. Williams?"

"I would welcome it."

They paused before entering the market and Kadiri lifted up a request. "Dear Heavenly Father, I ask for you to intercept the people who have taken Mrs. Williams, keep her safe, give the officers wisdom in their search and give peace to Mr. Williams. I ask in the holy name of your son, Jesus, amen."

George's phone rang. "Excuse me. Hello. Anthony, what's wrong? — No, you and the girls cannot come help look for Millie. How did you know she was missing?" George looked at Kadiri. "Sam called Jeremiah to let him know what was going on." About that time, a group of older tourists brushed past laughing. "No, it is too dangerous for you. You might be recognized as being related to Millie. You would be in danger or if you were taken, you could be used as leverage against her. – No, I'm telling you, you will be recognized as American's and you would be putting yourselves in danger. – What do you mean, you're sure you wouldn't be recognized?"

A man with a mustache and wearing a Panama hat tapped him on the shoulder. "Because even my own grandfather didn't recognize me."

George looked up in shock.

The girls, dressed as old ladies, sauntered up beside him and giggled. Becca said, "Now can we help look for Millie, Gramps? We love her too, you know."

Kadiri called Jaouhari for someone to escort the bold young people in their search. The officer quickly arrived and led the three disguised 'tourists' to the opposite side of the street to begin their search.

Chapter 18

In a Dark Room

Millie began to regain consciousness. The floor below her body was cool, she pushed herself up to a sitting position.

Here I am again, handcuffed, in a small, dimly lit room, but at least I don't have a hood over my head this time. Speaking of my head, it aches. I desperately needed a drink of water and I need to go to the bathroom. She looked around for anything that could help to free her from her bindings. *Think Millie, how can you cut these zip-ties? Father, give me wisdom, or give me strength, or both, in Jesus' name, amen.*

A rusty, metal cot stood next to the exterior wall. A thought popped into her mind. She scooted over to the bed. The smell of sweat and who-knows-what-else, attacked her nostrils. The odor of the filthy mattress nauseated her, but she forced herself to rest her ribs against the frame and place her right elbow onto the cot. With smooth, even strokes she scrapped the zip-ties along the edge of the jagged metal, a raspy noise accompanied the work. To cover the telltale sound, she began to sing—loudly, as she dragged the zip-tie along the rail. "He is the king of Kings!" A high note on that last word gave her the pep she needed.

Another long scratch at the plastic cuffs produced the next line of the impromptu song. “And to the cross I cling.”

Yet another long stroke at the bedframe generated the following line with that same high note at the end. “He is my every-thing.”

A low, almost base tone, in a descending cascade followed. “To Him I give all praise.”

She encouraged herself. “Round two, Millie! Here we go.” She belted it out. “He is the king of Kings!”

Scraaape.

“And to the cross I cling.”

Scratchhhh.

“He is my every-thing.”

Scr—at—ch. “To Him I give all praise.”

Scrape—Ping! The zip-tie broke.

“Now for a bathroom.” Using the same metal bed-frame she pushed herself up to her knees, which caused her body to lean over the revolting smelling mattress, but she paused. “Father, thank you for this cot that you provided and for its usefulness. Forgive me for not being more thankful and help me get out of this mess, but if I stand up, I’m going to pee all over myself. What should I do? In Jesus’ name, sir, amen.”

Toward the back of the room a ray of light shone onto a crate. The lid was slightly up at one corner. She pushed herself to a crouched position, waddled to the wooden box, shoved the lid aside, there nested in some straw, a large piece of pottery gave her an idea. She pulled up her nightgown, lowered her underwear and placed her fanny on the nice flat rim. “Ahhhhh! Thank you, Lord!” Something between a whizzing and tinkling sound produced much relief. The paper tag marked, *Antiquities*, provided the drying material. "Oh my! I hope this isn't expensive!" She wrestled her underwear to the proper place, brushed her gown to its full length and headed for the door.

Outside, Tony called George's phone. "Gramps, we heard Millie. She was singing. Come between the Saffron Hotel and the building to its west."

Chapter 19

From Outside

George and Kadiri quickly joined the three young people.

"I'm telling you, Gramps, we heard Millie's voice, in this alley, we just can't tell which way it came from. Shouldn't we shout her name?"

George rubbed his chin. "What did she say, Tony?"

"She was singing!"

Kadiri's eyebrows arched. "Singing? I wonder if that means she's still drugged?"

Becca leaned toward her gramps. "Shouldn't you call her?"

Kadiri placed his hand on George's arm. "Perhaps you should sing. Maybe no one would suspect a casual song as being a signal."

George searched his memory banks, his eyes brightened and he began to sing. "Oh, carry my loved one home safely to me. She sailed at the dawning, all day I've been blue. Red sails in the sunset, I'm trusting in you."[iii]

Shell clamped her hands together. "That should get her attention, Gramps."

Millie's voice responded. "George! George! Is that you?"

He placed his hands on a wall. "Millie, where are you?"

"I'm in a dim room somewhere near you, I think, unless I'm delirious."

George shouted, "Millie pound on the wall with your fist."

Thud, thud, thud came from their right.

"I think I know where you are. Be patient, Kadiri's here with me."

Kadiri lifted his phone to his ear. "Jaouhari, we've found her. We are between the buildings, behind the Saffron, she's in a room, we can't reach her from this side, can you get some men to the rear entrance?"

A frantic yell, interrupted the moment. "Get away from me! Stop! My husband and the police are outside. George! Yell!"

George placed his hands on the wall, as if trying to press through. "Stop it! Let her go!"

Tony, Becca and Shell joined in. "Leave her alone! We'll get you for this."

The slam of a door on the other side of the building, split the momentary clamor, then the sound of a commotion of many feet.

Her voice sounded relieved. "George, he's gone! The police just burst into the room. I'm safe. Are the kids with you? Or am I still drugged?"

"Yes, they're with me. We're coming around for you. We'll be there in a second." He, the three disguised young people and Kadiri dashed from the alley toward the back street just as the officers, one on each side holding her arms to steady her, ushered Millie outside. George lunged in and embraced her. She went limp in his arms and he lowered her to a seated position on the steps. An officer handed George a bottle of water. "Take a sip of this, my darling." He held the bottle to her lips, tipping it up slowly.

She gulped in the water, then following a long sigh, she said, "Thank you, my love." She glanced at the three in disguise. "What are you old folks doing here?"

They laughed in relief. "Looking for you G'momma." She smiled at the young people, then her eyebrows narrowed together and she looked up at Kadiri and Jaouhari. "We need to talk."

Jaouhari offered. "Let's get you back to the station, then we can talk."

Her head twisted side-to-side. "No, we need to talk now, get me into a police car, just you two and George. And have an officer escort these three, hmmm, tourists, back to the ship."

Tony interrupted, "But G'Millie we want to stay with you."

"You can't! He knows you! You would be in danger."

Tony and the girls' mouths dropped open. They nodded and Shell added, "Yes, ma'am, G'Millie."

Kadiri called his drive and discretely instructed him to see the three young people all the way to the deck of the *Princess of the Med.*

Once they were underway, Jaouhari led the way to his car and directed two officers to keep watch at either end of the vehicle, but to stand far enough away that they couldn't hear the conversation.

The two men complied.

From the backseat Millie leaned on George, but directed her comments to Kadiri and Jaouhari who twisted in the front seat to be able to face her.

"Messieurs, I have no proof of this, but I am suspicious of Saunders. The day of the incident in the market, before the merchant accused me, Saunders was speaking with a man nearby. I had to call him over to help me communicate with the stall keeper, then when I was being arrested, I caught a glimpse of the man with the eyepatch. He grinned at me as I was being led away."

Jaouhari rested his arms on the back of the seat. "You did not mention this at the station when I was interviewing you, Madame."

"Yes, Senior Sergeant, but remember when I told you I had a message for Monsieur Kadiri, then I changed my mind, I wasn't sure at that point who to trust. Maybe if I had trusted you with the information, I could have avoided being kidnapped *again.*"

Jaouhari smiled. "Perfectly understandable, Mrs. Williams, I too have become suspicious of Saunders, but as you say, I have no proof. Nevertheless, I have launched an investigation into his background."

Millie nodded. "Another point against him, Jaouhari is that no one, other than Saunders, you and your officers knew where we would be staying last night, but for now, I wish to go to the police station, pick up Saunders and go to court."

George straightened. "Millie, you can't! It's too dangerous!"

"Nonsense George, I must, now more than ever and we shan't let on a dibble that we suspect Saunders. It will be court as he had planned, only, please have more men on standby, just in case," she smiled. "I won't even bother to change out of my night gown, just procure me a shawl to throw over the top. That will make it look more like daywear."

Kadiri smiled back. "I think we can do better than that." He stepped from the squad car to a stall.

Millie saw him pick out an item and pay for it.

He returned to the vehicle and handed a garment over the seat.

She held it up by the shoulders. A most beautiful vibrant blue caftan with silver braid at the front stretched out before her. "Oh, Alif! It's stunning!" She peaked around the fabric and smiled. "Now get me to court."

Jaouhari called for the driver and they roared away from the market.

On the way, he radioed that Mrs. Williams was safe and Mr. and Mrs. Fielding and Saunders were to meet them at the courthouse.

It took only minutes to reach the building where the Tribunal was to take place. Saunders stood outside. He opened the rear car door and offered his hand. "Mrs. Williams, I'm so glad that you are unharmed. Are you sure you want to go through with this?"

She reached to hug him. "Certainly, Bryan, that's why I'm here, now, show me the way please, my good man."

When they entered the courtroom, the size of the room echoed their footsteps. A balcony of on-lookers stretched across the back, upper story of the room. Drab gray walls highlighted several international flags behind the area where the judges sat. The Tribunal had already begun, but Saunders stepped forward to address the court. "Secretary-General, as you know, I'm Bryan

Saunders, the Interpol Representative, please forgive our delay. This witness," He turned and pointed toward Millie, "had been kidnapped and only moments ago was rescued by local police."

The Secretary-General nodded. "Very well, thank you, Mr. Saunders," then addressed the National Prosecutor. "Mr. Prosecutor, you may call the witness."

Saunders turned to Millie. "Okay, Mrs. Williams, here we go." He walked her to the stand where she was sworn in, then took her seat in the witness box. Saunders returned to a table and seated himself.

TROUBLE IN MARRAKESH

Chapter 20

Her Testimony

The National Prosecution Attorney began, “Please state your name for the court.”

“I’m Mildred Williams, formerly Mildred Butterfly for the purpose of this hearing.”

The Prosecutor continued. “Can you tell us how you came to be involved,” He turned and swept his hand toward the defendant, “with Mr. Ferdinand Modesto?”

“Yes, my sister and I,” she glanced into the gallery in the balcony where Abby, Sam and George sat with Jaouhari, “we met Mr. Modesto on a cruise ship, on the *Princess of the Sea,* he was a conman posing as a passenger.”

The defense attorney jumped to his feet. “I object.”

In response, the Secretary-General glared at him. “Please sit down, sir,” then turned to the witness box, “and Mrs. Williams, will you reframe from stating your conclusions regarding the defendant? Simply tell us the facts not your personal judgments.”

Millie glanced at him. “Yes, sir, I’m sorry.”

The prosecutor continued, “Please, go on, Mrs. Williams.”

She looked at Ferdinand. “He was actually trying to con my sister and me out of money.”

Again, the defense attorney sprang to his feet. "I object."

Millie stared at him with one eyebrow raised, but the prosecutor carried on. "We're sorry, Secretary-General. Now Mrs. Williams, what led you to believe that Mr. Modesto was trying to con you and your sister out of money?"

"On a couple of outings ashore, he had," she made air-quotes, "conveniently forgotten his wallet, so my sister paid for a two-hour sailboat tour of the shore for the three of us and later he needed money for cab fare. Following that, at dinner one evening, he was supposed to be holding my sister's credit card for safety, but we witnessed him pulling the card from his pocket and paying for a meal with it, we learned later that, with tip, it cost over $300.00."

The attorney glanced at her. "And how did you learn of Mr. Modesto's involvement in the theft of the yacht, the Amelia Rose?"

Millie folded her arms and leaned back in the witness chair. "On one outing, Mr. Modesto, I believe, attempted to get us drunk, but I turned the tables on him. I didn't drink anything and allowed him, after he had finished two drinks, and half of my sister's, to drink one of mine also." She frowned. "It was then that he started blabbing about all of his exploits, including his involvement in the theft of the Amelia Rose." She glanced at Ferdinand who hung his head.

The prosecutor smiled at her. "Thank you, Mrs. Williams, no further questions at this time."

Ferdinand's defense lawyer stepped forward. "Mrs. Williams isn't it true that you got Mr. Modesto drunk and put words in his mouth which you later turned into a supposed charge against him to get him arrested," he whipped around to face her, "because you were jealous of his affection for your sister?"

In the gallery, Abby's hands spring to her mouth, but Millie remained composed and drew her shoulders back. "That is not true at all."

The defense attorney stepped toward the witness stand. "Didn't you charge a huge bill of swimsuits against his credit card?"

"Well, yes, I did, but it was to teach him a lesson."

Another step closer. "Was the lesson to punish him for preferring your sister over you?"

Millie bristled. "No, he was conning my sister and me out of money, so I turned the tables on him."

He reached the edge of the witness box. "Out of revenge, Mrs. Butterfly-Williams?"

"No, I was angry, but it was to teach him a lesson."

The defense attorney placed his hands on the edge of the box. "So, you are a teacher of moral lessons?" He glanced up at the Tribunal panel. "Does that include getting him drunk?"

"Now wait just a minute, Buster."

The Secretary-General's deadpan voice interrupted. "Just answer the question, Mrs. Williams."

She turned her head his direction. "How can I answer a question that is incorrect and an accusation?"

Leaning forward the Secretary-General said, "There is no Fifth Amendment here, Mrs. Williams, just answer the question."

Millie paused and pressed her eyes shut. *Lord, direct my words.* She opened her eyes and continued. "After we bought our swimsuits, we went to the beach. My sister and I walked around in the water a little bit, then went back to the chaise lounges that Mr. Modesto had procured. After being in the sun, we were both thirsty, so Ferdinand *kindly* offered to get drinks for us. He knew neither of us drank alcoholic beverages, but he ordered three, quart-sized, alcoholic, fruit drinks called Sunrises. I figured he was up to something so I didn't drink mine. Unfortunately, I wasn't able to warn my sister without tipping my hand to Mr. Modesto."

"So, you admit you were tricking him?"

"No, I was simply trying not to let him know that I knew he was trying to trick us. And, as I was saying, after half the glass, my sister was asleep because she was not used to drinking alcohol, so Ferdinand drank his and the rest of hers. I had poured mine into the sand. I asked him if he thought we should stop, but he said, 'no,' so the bartender brought another for him and one for me."

The defense attorney scowled at her. "Therefore, it is safe to say that you encouraged him to continue drinking."

"Nooo, as I said, I gave him the opportunity to stop drinking!"

The defense attorney turned to scan the gallery of people in the balcony. "But you allowed him to continue drinking?"

Millie leaned forward and her shoulders shot back tight. "I am neither his mother, nor his conscience. I allowed him to make the decision for himself." She glanced up to the balcony. George sat on the front row, leaning forward on the rail, with Abby, Sam and Jaouhari alongside him. That gave her momentum to continue. "After he consumed his second Sunrise and again, I mention the other half of my sister's, he drank my second one as well."

The defense attorney's eyes diverted from the gallery back to the witness stand. "So, you got him drunk?"

"No, sir," she leaned forward more, "he got himself drunk because he was a glutton! And by that time, he was very chatty," her eyes glared at the barrister.

The attorney folded his arms and leaned in. "And this is when you confused Mr. Modesto and put words in his mouth which you later twisted, into a fraudulent confession?"

Millie smiled and relaxed her shoulders, she glanced up to the Tribunal panel, then back to the defense counsel. "No, sir, Mr. Modesto had told us on a prior occasion, when he was not drinking, I might add, that his business was in acquisitions. At this point, I merely asked what types of things he acquired. He very proudly boasted about his exploit of helping to seize the Amelia Rose, as well as stealing a priceless painting, which was later found in his apartment in London, along with several other valuables that Interpol was interested in. It is the Amelia Rose that has brought me here today, because due to his actions and the actions of others, some crewmembers suffered injuries. If I had not come to testify, my testimony at the time of his arrest would have been considered hearsay evidence."

The defense attorney turned to face his client, but spoke to Millie. "Did Mr. Modesto say that he took the crew hostage?"

Millie scrunched her eyebrows and shook her head. "No, he was very clear that he was not involved in that portion of the theft."

The attorney jerked around to face her again. "Then

why are you out-to-get Mr. Modesto put into prison?"

She straightened. "I am not *out-to-get Mr. Modesto put into prison*, as you put it, sir. It is Interpol that is out-to-get him put into prison, for the troubles he has been involved in. They want Ferdinand, I mean, Mr. Modesto, to identify the thieves who did take the crew hostage. Interpol is hoping that my testimony will be the weight that causes him to turn-in the ones who hired him." She smiled at Ferdinand. "And I hope he will."

With arms still folded, one of the defense attorney's eyebrows shot up. "Why is that your interest, Mrs. Williams."

She glared at him. "Because, in my travels to this court meeting, I survived an explosion, which was meant to kill me *and* my sister who was traveling with me, as well as the fact that I was drugged last night, kidnapped and held hostage up until only moments before I walked into this courtroom. The men behind this particular crime are vicious, ruthless and need to be apprehended."

His jaw dropped and he stuttered. "No more questions."

The Secretary-General's monotony voice replied, "You may step down, Mrs. Williams."

She stepped from the witness box, walked to the table where Saunders sat and seated herself next to him.

Saunders' leaned back with his arms folded across his chest, his hands rested atop the bends of his elbows, he whispered to her, "Good job, Mrs. Williams."

The Prosecutor called his next witness. "Secretary-General, I would like to call Mr. Alaoui to the stand, please."

A dry voice rose from the Tribunal Directors bench.

"Mr. Alaoui, please approach the stand."

Chapter 21

Expert Witness

The National Prosecution Attorney addressed his witness. "Mr. Alaoui, what qualifies you as an expert in the area of oceans, seas and currents?"

"I have lived all of my life on the coastal areas of Morocco. At age eight, I set sail with my father on a shipping freighter. As I realize now, following the death of my mother, he had no choice but to take me with him in an effort to keep me close and protect me. He had me at the helm with him every minute that he was there. He talked of currents, wind and weather continually, by age twelve, he said I was as proficient as any sailor that he knew. It was only natural for me, at age eighteen, to captain a ship of my own. Much later, of course, I was approached to serve on the board of the National Shipping Association to help train a new generation of men and women."

The Prosecutor asked, "As the now, Director of the National Shipping Association of Morocco, what can you tell us about the currents and their impact on the crew of the yacht Amelia Rose?"

"Well, sir, the currents off the Atlantic coast of Morocco are much different than those on the

Mediterranean side of the country. For instance, taking a sailing vessel from Tangier into the Mediterranean Sea would provide a current drawing the vessel along the coast, but the so-called merchants, with whom Mr. Modesto worked, were unskilled in sailing in the open ocean. They captured the vessel outside the coastal waters off Safi and when they set the crew adrift in a lifeboat, rather than the small vessel being pulled toward shore, it was pushed out to sea, in a southerly direction."

The prosecutor asked, "Would setting the crew adrift on that coast of the nation, in your professional opinion, be a dangerous act?"

"Definitely, sir. It is fortunate that the crew were found as soon as they were, but having been adrift for nearly two days under the scorching sun with no fresh water and only their shirts tied together and held aloft to shade them, it's a miracle that they were alive."

"Thank you, Mr. Alaoui, is there anything else you would like to add?"

"Yes, I would like to say that it is this kind of greed, arrogance, and stupidity that costs good, hardworking sailors their lives. If they are convicted of nothing else, their stupidity should be enough to send them to prison."

The Advocate for Ferdinand stood. "I object. This is a personal opinion based on nothing more than Mr. Alaoui's bias."

The Prosecutor turned. "Again, thank you Mr. Alaoui." He looked at Ferdinand's attorney. "Your witness, counselor."

The Advocate stood. "Mr. Alaoui, do you agree that your last statement was based on emotion and your own personal bias?"

The witness looked into the eyes of the Advocate. "Yes, sir, it is emotional and it is based on the hundreds of deaths I have seen over the sixty years that I've sailed. And over the greed and foolishness that I've witnessed leading to many of those deaths. It is emotional to look into the faces of widows and orphans and tell them that their loved one is not coming home because some greedy businessman or filthy criminal has cost them their life." He stared directly at Ferdinand Modesto but addressed the attorney. "Yes sir, it is emotional."

With wide eyes, the attorney said, "No more questions for this witness," he straightened his back, looked up at the Tribunal Council and continued, "but your honor, may I call Ferdinand Modesto to the stand?"

Chapter 22

Ferdinand on the Stand

The Tribunal director responded. “Mr. Modesto, will you take the stand please.”

Ferdinand inched from his chair, stood erect and buttoned his jacket. He walked to the witness box, entered and faced his attorney.

The director addressed him. “Mr. Modesto, do you swear to tell the whole truth?”

Ferdinand nodded. “I do, sir.”

“You may be seated.”

He lowered himself into the chair, as his advocate approached. “Mr. Modesto, will you tell the Tribunal what happened on the day the yacht, the Amelia Rose was stolen?”

He fidgeted for a moment, then began. “Miss Amelia and I had taken the train from Safi, where the yacht was docked, to Ben Guerir, from there we boarded the train for Marrakesh, where Amelia wished to do some shopping. When we arrived, she told me she would only be a few minutes and entered a shop, but I knew from experience that she would be distracted for a couple of hours or more, so as I had planned, I rented a car, drove the two and a half hours back to Safi and boarded the yacht. No one was at the gangway when I returned, they were playing cards in the crew's quarters, as was their usual habit when their mistress was ashore."

The Advocate leaned forward. "What did you do then?"

"I located the room where the game was being held and knocked on the doorframe of the open door. I told the captain that Amelia had changed her mind and now wished to sail to Greece."

"What was his response?"

"He immediately set off for the bridge and told the crew to prepare to sail. During their hurried preparation, I again escaped to the dock and hid, just before the gangway was pulled aboard."

The Advocate glanced up at the gentlemen of the Tribunal panel, then back to Ferdinand. "So, Mr. Modesto, you had no part in the actual theft of the yacht, nor of stranding the sailors at sea?"

Ferdinand nodded. "That is correct."

The Advocate turned to the prosecutor. "Your witness." He arrogantly strolled back to his seat, smiling.

The Prosecutor, a short, stout, unassuming man, stomped to the witness box. "Mr. Modesto, am I correct, in gathering from your testimony that you had no part whatsoever in the theft of the Amelia Rose or the stranding of her crew?"

Ferdinand sat straight. "Yes, that is correct."

The Prosecutor turned to face the advocate, Mr. Saunders and Millie, then lifted his gaze to scan the onlookers in the balcony. "No part whatsoever," he paused, "except being hired by a criminal gang," he paused again, then turned to face Ferdinand, "agreeing to deliver the yacht into their hands, deceiving the owner, stranding her alone in Marrakesh, secretly returning to the yacht, giving false orders to the captain, then scurrying to the dock to hide like a rat, as the captain and crew of the Amelia Rose sailed, without knowing it, into a hijacking. Is that what you call 'no part whatsoever,' Mr. Modesto?"

The Advocate jumped to his feet. "I object?"

The director of the Tribunal leaned forward. "You object to what, sir?"

He tilted his head toward the tribunal's director. "The Prosecutor is testifying, your honor."

The director folded his arms. "Is he testifying truthfully or falsely, sir?"

The advocate lowered himself into his seat.

The Prosecutor smiled. "Thank you, Secretary General," and turned his gaze back to Ferdinand. "Will you answer the question, Mr. Modesto? Is that what you call 'no part whatsoever'?"

Ferdinand's head drooped forward.

Continuing with a grin, the Prosecutor said, "I'll take that as an admission of guilt, Mr. Modesto. Now, I have been instructed to offer you an opportunity to reduce your sentence if you will name the person or persons who hired you to commit the act of sending the yacht Amelia Rose into the hands of these merciless hijackers." He turned to face the gallery again. "What say ye, Mr. Modesto? Are the hijackers present? Is your employer present? Or can you give the Tribunal their names?"

With an almost simultaneous inhale of air, the gallery of people in the balcony gasped!

The Prosecutor turned to the sight of Modesto's head tipped back, his body slumped in the chair and a large dart lodged in the front of his throat, the attorney's jaw dropped.

Another commotion in the gallery forced him to wheel around, as Millie jumped to her feet and pointed to the far end of the balcony. "That's him, Jaouhari! The man with the eyepatch."

Jaouhari sprang to his feet and shouted, "After him, men! Catch him!"

But the one-eyed man leapt over the rail of the balcony and landed as effortlessly as a cat, on the courtroom floor. From a crouched position he rose and covered the distance between himself and Millie in mere seconds.

George stumbled down the balcony stairs, but stiffened when he saw a sharp blade against Millie's pale neck.

A low guttural growl came forth. "If you want this woman back alive, stay where you are!" With the knife in front of her throat, he pressed his chest against her back and dragged her to the door, turning his head and shifting his one good eye side-to-side to guard the path. He leaned against the door and it swung open into the hallway. Guards jumped to their feet, but he repeated his demand. "Nobody, move!"

Jaouhari and Kadiri eased through an adjoining doorway as the man propelled Millie backwards down the corridor.

Jaouhari raised his hand and in French yelled, "Stand fast, men, allow him to pass." He lifted his voice higher toward the perpetrator. "Sir, let the woman go."

"I might … when I'm safely out of this country.

Tell your men to give me a car."

Giving the man a wide berth, Jaouhari slipped along the farthest wall toward the front door. He opened it and shouted, "Officers, a man is coming out with a knife to Mrs. William's throat. Make no sudden moves, stand back and allow him to take my car."

"Wise move, Senior Sergeant, now you stay here and make sure your men obey." He pushed Millie out in front of him toward the car at the curb. "Open the door, fat camel."

Millie flinched. "Who are you calling a fat camel, you scuzz-bag?" She twisted to peer over her shoulder.

He grinned to show his yellow, uneven teeth. "Zip it, cow." He opened the door, lowered the knife, pushed Millie in and shouted, "slide across the seat." He slid in behind her, "no sudden moves, do you hear me?"

She nodded.

He slammed the door and reached for the key that dangled in the ignition, fired up the engine and the vehicle screeched away from the curb.

Millie glanced around. "Where are you taking me?"

"Quiet!"

She bristled and pushed her back away from the seat and turned her shoulders to face him. "I will not be quiet, where are you taking me?"

"We're going to the coast to find a boat, now shut up!"

Easing her body against the seat, in a soft voice, she prayed. "No weapon formed against me will prosper, this is my heritage as a servant of the Lord."[iv]

He growled at her. "Shut up, I said!"

She faced him and shouted. "There shall no evil befall me, God has given his angels charge over me.[v]"

He laughed. "Evil has already befallen you, you infidel, Allah has delivered you into my hands."

Millie put one hand on the dashboard, the other on the back of the seat and turned her body to address him. "Have you not seen the power of my God? He delivered me from the train explosion. He delivered me from the hands of a jailer last night and from the bonds of kidnappers this morning and you shall see how he will deliver me from you."

In a flash, the back of his hand caught her cheek. "Why didn't he deliver you from that?" A cruel laugh escaped his lips accompanied by foul breath.

She cradled her cheek with her hand. "God never said that we wouldn't have tribulation, but he *will* deliver me. You cannot take my life." She stared at the side of his face and asked, "Are you Balthazar?"

A roar of laughter burst forth, his garlicy breath again filled the air. "Balthazar is a myth; do you not know that fat camel?"

His teeth shown, smoke-stained yellow in the sunlight. "Balthazar is a ghost, so far away that no one can touch him, yet close enough that you might grab his arm."

Her eyes stretched wide. "So, you know him then?"

He snarled and his shiny, eye-patch met her gaze. "As do you, stupid American cow!" Without warning, the side of his fist caught her forehead, her head slammed back and hit the window.

Darkness!

Chapter 23

Darkness to Light

Seagulls squawking rousted Millie from darkness into a dream-like haze and a massive headache. “Where am I?” No one responded. “George?” She placed her hands on her temples. “Oh, my head,” she tried to focus. “Lord, where am I?” The answer came in the form of clarity. “Yes, thank you Lord, I remember now.” She glanced at the driver’s seat, it was empty, she tried to open her door, but it was locked. “Lord, I need your help and guidance.”

The sound of the driver’s door opening drew her attention.

“Ahhh, I see the camel has awakened, just in time to walk, so that I don’t have to hire a cart to carry your fat body.” He cackled. “I’ve found a ship heading out in minutes. You will accompany me to Greece where you will once again meet Balthazar.”

She stared into his face. “I don’t think so, scuzz-ball, no matter what you think.”

His cruel laughter sickened her. “You are a feisty cow, but no match for my strength. Now slide across the seat to me.”

She used the back of the seat and the steering wheel to drag herself toward him.

He leaned in to grab her arm. "Hurry up, stupid woman."

The heel of her right hand pushed toward his face, but he knocked it away and pulled a knife from his back pocket. "I don't have to kill you, I'm not being paid for that, but you *will* come with me as my shield." He grabbed her left arm and dragged her toward the open door, which forced her caftan up above her knees. When her left leg came out of the car, he yanked her, forcing her off balance, but her foot reached the ground.

Her voice grew bolder. "No—weapon—formed—against me will prosper! In Jesus' name!"

A slur of disgust followed. "Your Jesus is a pagan god," he straightened his back and lifted his chin. "Allah will guide me to victory."

Staring into his one good eye, she shouted, "Allah-shmallah!"

His lips parted and his eye opened wide.

Her right leg flew from inside the car, catching him forcefully between the legs. "Whose God is a pagan god now?"

He drooped to his knees, his mouth sagged open, but only garbled utterances escaped.

Standing next to the kneeling man, she closed her eyes, reared back and swung with a haymaker.

Thud!

Her hand throbbed from the impact, she clutched it to her chest and hopped around groaning, "Ow, ow, ow!" Then noticed the man's flattened body and leaned over him. "I told you no weapon formed against me would prosper."

Two police cars swerved into the parking lot and skidded to a stop. Doors flung open. Jaouhari, Kadiri,

George, Saunders, and two young officers leapt from the vehicles and ran toward her.

George tried to embrace her, but she pushed him aside and dashed toward Kadiri, she whirled around, grabbed Saunders by the wrist and said, "'Yet close enough that you may grab his arm.' It's him, Kadiri, it's Saunders. He's Balthazar."

Saunders brows shot up and his eyes popped open. "What? Dear lady, the strain must have been too much for you."

She turned her gaze to Jaouhari. "I saw him give a signal in the courtroom. His right hand lay atop his left arm, he glanced into the gallery of people and lifted his right index finger."

Kadiri's eyes met hers. "Are you sure it wasn't just an involuntary action?"

She faced Saunders again and pulled her shoulders back. "No, it was voluntary, I'm sure. As he lifted his finger, my eyes followed the direction of the not-so-innocent flick to where I saw this eye-patched-man," she pointed to the thug on the ground, "he slid from his chair, dashed to the rail and leapt over. It all makes sense now. Saunders has been in on this from the start and I believe he's Balthazar." She pointed to the unconscious felon again. "And he told me, 'Balthazar is a ghost, so far away that no one can touch him, yet close enough that you might grab his arm.'"

Kadiri lowered his chin to his chest and stepped toward Saunders.

Saunders took a step back. "This is a mistake, or the woman is crazy. I'm a representative of Interpol, they've fully vetted me, I'm the one who brought Modesto here for trial. I'm the one after Balthazar."

Kadiri grasped him by the upper arm. “Come with me Saunders, we’ll sort this out at the station.”

Millie reached for George and pulled him close. “I’m sorry I pushed you away, darling, but I needed to get to Kadiri.”

George wrapped his arms around her. “It’s okay, my love,” he paused, “justice first, I completely understand,” then he smiled.

She leaned in and kissed his cheek. “How did you find me?”

“Jaouhari’s squad car has a tracking device. We were only minutes behind you, all the way, but I was still worried. Are you okay?”

The corners of Millie’s mouth eased up. “I’m fine, just a headache. I got bopped against the window and knocked out for most of the trip.”

Kadiri walked up. “I hate to interrupt, Mr. and Mrs. Williams, but will you accompany us once again to the station in Marrakesh?”

George grabbed his arm. “We need to get Millie checked out first, that thug knocked her unconscious.”

Kadiri turned to his driver. “Call for an ambulance and an extra transport vehicle, Sergeant.”

After the medics checked Millie over and gave her the all-clear, the unconscious thug was checked and handcuffed, then Jaouhari motioned for drivers and sent Saunders, also handcuffed and the now conscious, eye-patched man ahead in separate vehicles along with armed escorts.

Chapter 24

The Return Trip

Millie, George and Kadiri, entered the remaining squad car, Senior Sergeant Jaouhari climbed behind the wheel for their return drive to Marrakesh. He radioed ahead, "Sergeant, be on alert, two maximum security prisoners are on their way and inform Mrs. Fielding that her sister is safe and well."

When they arrived at the station, Saunders' voice echoed in the sparsely furnished room, as officers led him, struggling, to a holding cell. "This is a mistake. The woman has gone mad, I'm telling you, check with Interpol, I have a sterling reputation."

As Millie and George came through the tall double doors of the station, Abby and Sam rushed at them.

Abby threw her arms around her sister's neck. "My goodness, it's so good to have you back. Are you okay? I can't believe the things you've been through."

Millie laughed. "Let me breath, Abby, you're choking me."

She gasped and pushed away. "I'm so sorry."

Millie wrapped her arms around Abby. "I'm only teasing, dear. I'm fine. You weren't hurting me."

"Oh, for goodness' sakes, Millie!" Abby let out a

long push of air. "Do be serious. I've been worried sick about you. When I saw that eye-patch-man grab you, I nearly fainted."

Millie chuckled. "Me too, but God assured me He was in control. When that guy started calling Jesus a false god, I knew that it was only a matter of time before the Lord set him straight—and he did—straight out flat in the parking lot." Her laughter echoed in the room.

Jaouhari walked up. "I heard it was the woman infidel that flattened him. He's saying that you are a witch and you used your witchcraft on him, otherwise you would never have been able to overtake him," and the Senior Sergeant laughed.

With another burst of laughter, Millie turned to Jaouhari. "Isn't his god strong enough to overcome the witchcraft of an infidel?"

He leaned in. "Not so loud, there are good men around here that believe in Allah, they just haven't found the truth yet. Don't give them any further cause to resist the witness of the Holy Spirit."

She whispered back. "Sorry, I see your point. How did you come to know the Lord, Jaouhari?"

"My grandmother was the housekeeper of a Christian missionary. She had been warned by her imam to be on guard against his words."

"So how did he break through her defenses?"

Jaouhari smiled. "He did not, but his ten-year-old daughter caught my grandmother off-guard and led her to Christ."

"That's amazing! Out of the mouth of babes, according to Psalm eight, verse two."

"Yes, indeed. After receiving Jesus, grandmother

took the child, with her father's permission, to meet the imam. As he tried to convert the child to Islam, she gave such good arguments against his statements that he agreed to meet with her father. After his conversion to Christianity, a mighty revival broke out."

George wrapped his arms around Millie. "Perhaps we will see another revival as a result of Millie's mighty right arm," and he chuckled.

Chief Inspector Kadiri approached. "That would be a welcomed outcome, Madam Millie." The group turned their attention to him as he continued. "You might not yet know, but after Modesto's death and Millie's kidnapping, the Tribunal went into recess. They thought their case had come to an end, but Millie, once you were found and pointed the blame to Saunders, I notified the Tribunal panel. They are doing a deep background check on Bryan Saunders, but wish to hear your testimony against him. Are you up to it?"

Abby tapped Kadiri on the arm. "Hasn't my sister been through enough, monsieur? Can't you handle it from here?"

"I truly wish it were that simple, dear lady, but my evidence would again be hearsay, without your sister's corroboration."

George pulled Millie close and turned her to stare into her eyes. "Before you say anything, I'm sure no one would think badly of you if you decided not to testify. Please think about what is best for yourself for a change."

She kissed his cheek. "Oh George, my love, what is best for me—and you—and Abigail and everyone I love, is to get that beast off of the streets. I truly believe that Saunders, yes, wrinkled clothes, meek Mr.

Saunders, is Balthazar. His thieving was internationally known for years, but now he is leaving a trail of bodies."

Jaouhari interrupted. "And on that note, the body of the young hotel clerk was found this morning in an alley near the Saffron Hotel."

Abby threw her hands to her chest and gasped. "Oh no, he was such a sweet young man."

Millie turned to her husband. "See George, will I, or you, or Abby, or any of our family be safe if I'm right and he's set free?"

George's head tipped forward and air rushed past his lips. "I guess you're right, but I am not leaving your side until this is over and done with."

She nodded. "Agreed, but what about your Board of Director's Meetings?"

"Jeremiah will take my place and text me any questions he has or any vote that is needed. The other members agreed to this arrangement, under the circumstances."

Millie turned to Kadiri. "Tell his majesty the high court, tribunal, justice-whoever, that I'll see him in the morning. Now, can I get something to eat that won't knock me out?"

Jaouhari laughed. "I think I can manage that. Let's get you, Mr. Williams, Dr. and Mrs. Fielding settled at the hotel. My grandmother is cooking Kababs this afternoon. She always makes enough for an army, so Chief Inspector Kadiri, if he doesn't mind, and I will personally bring us all a feast and we can go over your testimony for tomorrow's Tribunal."

Kadiri nodded. "Sounds wonderful."

Millie rubbed her hands together. "Yes, sounds

marvelous."

Chapter 25

Kababs

Kadiri arranged a table for six in Millie and George's suite. Four policemen were stationed in the hallway and given orders to bring their own food and drink for the evening and not to share a morsel with anyone. In that arrangement, if one person got drugged, the others should still be alert.

Lamb on skewers, served over rice with a homemade yogurt, sprinkled with fresh dill thrilled the taste buds of Millie, George, Abby, Sam, Kadiri and Jaouhari himself.

Millie leaned back in her chair. "George, we need to tell the Board of Directors to hire Senior Sergeant Jaouhari's grandmother as a backup chef for the *Princess of the Med*." Then suddenly she sat bolt-upright. "That reminds me, what happened to Bastien? Is he safe? Did he get back to the ship?"

Kadiri leaned forward to reassure her. "The lad has been found and is safe. It turns out, that the Tangier police were looking for him to determine whether he was involved in the train car explosion. When he was located, he explained that when he tried to return to the Observation Lounge with your drinks and the car was missing, he didn't know what to do, but he was afraid to return to the ship because his father had commissioned him with your safety. He feared his father's wrath at what his father would consider a 'monumental failure,' as he called it."

Abby clutched her hands to her chest. "Oh, I'm so glad he's okay. He's such a nice boy."

George smiled. "I would have been afraid of his father too, if I'd been him. Millie lavished her charm on Jean Claude one time and he was smitten."

With a shoulder-bump, Millie chuckled. "Oh George. Well, I'll have a talk with Jean Claude when we get back. No one can possibly believe it was the boy's fault, I'm just glad he's safe. By the way, where did they find him?"

Kadiri grinned. "He was at the train station in Casablanca, hiding amongst the bellmen as a porter for tips to buy food."

Abby's shoulders pulled back. "That must have been excruciating for him after eating his dad's marvelous food all of his life, surely Jean Claude will think that's punishment enough."

After a round of laughter, Jaouhari asked, "Mrs. Williams, may we make notes of all the reasons you believe that Saunders was involved in your stressful mishaps and why you believe he is Balthazar?"

"Certainly, do you have a notepad?"

Jaouhari pulled a pad from his pocket. "And I'm sure you will not mind if the Chief Inspector stays to hear your evidence?"

Millie smiled. "Alif is more than welcome to stay too."

Chapter 26

Reasons for Guilt

Millie tilted her head back. “I think it goes all the way back to our first meeting on the *Princess of the Sea*. When I first accused Ferdinand and he was arrested, afterwards I was kidnapped. The kidnappers sent a ransom note demanding the exact amount of money that Saunders had told me and Abby that we would receive for a reward for his capture.” She looked from Jaouhari to Alif. “Funny don’t you think that it was the exact amount of the reward we were granted. At first, I thought someone had overheard our conversation with Saunders, but now the evidence has mounted.”

Alif nodded. “Alone, that would be hard to prove, but continue please, Millie.”

Millie glanced at the Chief Inspector, “Well, after your concerns about our husbands and Jeremiah.”

George interrupted. “What!”

Alif smiled. “It was only a formality, Mr. Williams, please continue, Millie.”

Millie patted her husband’s arm. “Well, I guess I was more rattled than I realized, but later it dawned on me that Jeremiah had said he would notify the Interpol Liaison, which as you know is Saunders.”

Jaouhari made notes, but paused to look up. "And this was during the time you were unsure whether to trust me or not," and smiled.

"Yes, dear, I'm sorry, but then I remembered that after Alif found us, he also had Saunders notified that Abby and I were safe and on our way to Marrakesh. From the moment he boarded the ship in the Caribbean, Bryan Saunders was always in the loop."

George rubbed his chin. "You're right again, my lady." He looked at Kadiri and pointed at Millie with his thump, "this one is sharp as a tack."

Kadiri nodded. "I totally agree, Monsieur Williams, she is a remarkable woman."

Millie continued. "I even suspect that Ferdinand would never have made it to Marrikesh if the Caribbean Officer had not been travelling with them. Oh, and Saunders alone was to stand guard at the Saffron Hotel, but it would have been too suspicious I think to attack me there with Abby along, so he suggested we walk in the market, I was stupid not to realize how dangerous it was."

Jaouhari leaned forward. "You thought you were in the care of someone you could trust."

"Thank you, yes, but I should have been more alert. I began to suspect when we were in the market and Saunders had wandered away from us. I saw him across the street talking to someone when Abby called him to help me when shopping for a skirt and blouse for court. By the way, where are they? Oh, never mind."

Jaouhari chuckled. "I will have your clothing brought to you for court tomorrow, please continue."

"When the kerfuffle in the market happened, the eye-patched man was there. He smirked at me as I was being taken away. If it hadn't been for Abby's quick thinking and putting that coin in the cash box, this might have turned out very different."

Sam gave Abby a sideways hug. "That's my girl."

The notepad dropped to Jaouhari's lap. "I would hope, Madame, that my keen powers of police work would have gotten to the correct response either way, but a night in the cells would have protected you from being kidnapped again," then he smirked.

"Okay, cheeky monkey, you've done well by me and tell your grandmother that the dinner was delicious." She smiled, then it melted. "But perhaps if I had been locked up overnight that poor young man at the Marriot would still be alive."

Kadiri patted her arm. "Now Millie, that was not your fault. Let's focus on getting his killer put away. We are sure that it was the eye-patched man, his name is Driss Messaoudi and we are almost positive that Messaoudi shot the dart that killed Modesto in the courtroom, but we want to know who was giving the orders."

Millie rallied. "Yes, it was Saunders who signaled him to kill Ferdinand, I'm sure of that and then he signaled Messaoudi to run. Unfortunately, he saw his only way out was to take me hostage."

George scooted his chair over, touching hers, stretched his arm around her and pulled her close.

She cuddled close to her husband. "Jaouhari, when your officer checked us in at the Marriott, Saunders lagged behind when we were entering the elevator, but he didn't have enough time to tell the clerk to drug our food, so I don't know what he did and the food arrived before Saunders left the room with your officer, so we may be missing something there."

He nodded. "I'll check with our men and see if there is camera footage of the front desk for that evening when you checked in."

Millie leaned forward. "Oh, and I haven't thanked you for asking them to provide toothbrushes and night gowns for us."

Jaouhari straightened. "That wasn't me. I had an officer set up the reservation."

Kadiri turned to him. "Who was it? I want to talk to him."

Jaouhari pulled his cellphone from his pocket and dialed. "Yes, I want to talk to Officer Zirri." – "Have you tried to contact him?" – "Check CCTV for the night Mrs. Williams was brought in. Follow him on the video until after she is taken to the Marriott Hotel. Let me know what you find out and would you have someone bring Mrs. Williams clothes to the hotel?" He hung up. "While we are waiting, please continue your account, Mrs. Williams."

"It probably isn't worth mentioning, but the van that took the clerk from the Marriott, must have taken him to the area of the Saffron, because that's where his body was found and I was being held in a building behind that hotel, so that clerk, might be a lead."

His cellphone rang, Jaouhari answered. "Yes, I see, and that was his only contact before Mrs. Williams was taken to the hotel. And afterwards? – Yes, I see, good work Sergeant. And would you have an officer pick up the clerk at the Saffron Hotel and bring him in for questioning?" He rested the phone on the table. "It seems the only person to speak with our missing officer was Saunders, just before Mrs. Williams and Mrs.

Fielding were taken to the Marriott. After they left for the hotel, our man made a phone call. It will take some time to trace the call through our records with the phone exchange, but I think we can guess where he called. Saunders' *lag behind* time must have been to make sure the clerk had received the call and to threaten him. And that officer did not report for duty today and is not at home. We can only assume that he is *in the wind* as you Americans would say," and he smiled.

Millie leaned back against George again, sighed and said, "Unless he has been added to the body count."

A scowl covered Jaouhari's face. "Indeed, it would be regrettable, but so would prison be for anyone who betrayed his position. Things of that nature are dealt with swiftly and firmly in our police force."

The cellphone rang again, Jaouhari answered. "The clerk from the Saffron is in route to the station."

Millie laughed. "Bless his heart, he must be innocent or he would be dead or missing."

Kadiri nodded. "That would be a fair assumption, considering how things have ended for others who were involved, voluntarily or involuntarily."

Sam stood and reached for Abby's hand. "Millie, George, we will excuse ourselves and return to our room. Senior Sergeant Jaouhari, thank you for the delicious meal, we thank both you and the Chief Inspector for protecting Millie and Abby." He nodded to both gentlemen. "We'll say goodnight now," and they walked to the adjoining room and closed the door behind them.

Kadiri glanced at Jaouhari, "Perhaps we should leave also and allow this brave lady and her husband to get some rest."

Kadiri and Jaouhari stood. A tap on the door threw everyone's attention. Jaouhari stepped to the door. "Who's there?"

An unfamiliar language replied, but Jaouhari relaxed and opened the door.

An Officer stretched out a bag which the Senior Sergeant glanced into, thanked the man and closed the door again. He turned to Millie and smiled. "Here are your garments for tomorrow, Madame."

George stood and reached for the parcel, as Millie replied. "Thank you, Senior Sergeant."

Jaouhari nodded. "You are most welcome, Mrs. Williams and thank you for your help, I will type my notes and make a few copies, four to give to the Secretary General and the other members of the panel, a copy for you, one for the Chief Inspector and a copy for my file. I will pick you up personally for the hearing tomorrow, say eight o'clock."

"And," Kadiri added, "I shall accompany him, if that is satisfactory with you, Senior Sergeant."

"Perfectly so, Sir and goodnight, Mr. and Mrs. Williams."

George walked them to the door and locked it behind them. As an extra measure of safety, he dragged a chair in front of the door and propped it under the doorknob. He glanced at Millie, she was about to doze off in her chair, he rushed over. "Millie," he reached around her waist and helped her up. "Time to get some rest, I'll be right here, dear."

After helping her into bed and covering her up, he tapped on the adjoining door.

Sam opened it and whispered, "Abby's asleep, does Millie need a sedative?"

George stepped aside to allow Sam to see that she was already in bed. “No, I think she is worn-out and will sleep. I’ve placed a chair under the doorknob as a precaution. Perhaps you should do the same.” He smiled. “Goodnight, Sam, I love you and Abby so much.”

Chapter 27

Sudden Alarm

After an uneventful night, the two couples sat at the table in Millie and George's suite, eating a breakfast that Sam had gotten personally from the kitchen. A thud, thud, thud at the door caused them all to jump.

Jaouhari called out. "Mr. and Mrs. Williams, are you all right?"

George rushed to the door, moved the chair and cracked it open. "We're fine! What's going on?"

The Senior Sergeant pushed him back into the room, stepped inside and closed the door. "Saunders has escaped. It seems that our officer came in this morning pleading for mercy after missing his shift yesterday. He claimed to have been drugged the night before and just woke up this morning. The Desk Sergeant was checking with me, when a commotion broke out in the cells. When we investigated, we found that the man on cell duty had been knocked unconscious and Saunders had fled with the aid of our officer. We have teams out searching for them and a team outside this hotel, but I don't think you should leave your room."

Millie stood, wearing the skirt and blouse from the market. "Jaouhari, we have to finish this. Take me to the courthouse. Can you arrange a private meeting for me with the Tribunal heads?"

He shook his head and bristled. "I can't allow it!"

George jumped to his feet. "And I forbid it, Millie!"

She turned slowly to face her husband. "George, I will chalk that up to the fact that you're overwrought, but you might want to reconsider the way you phrased that."

He charged forward. "I will not! I love you and I won't risk your life again on this foolish mission. People have died, Millie, trying to put this man away. Please don't ask me to risk losing you!"

A tap on the door revealed Kadiri.

Jaouhari opened the door and Kadiri rushed in. "I assume you can't talk her out of it."

"That is correct, Chief Inspector. She insists on going to the courthouse. We can request a private meeting with the four Tribunal Council Members, behind closed doors."

Kadiri nodded. "Very well, but with no advanced warning. When we arrive, you can call the Secretary-General and tell him we are in the courthouse, then we will usher Millie into the private chambers behind the bench and request the panel to join us there.'

"Yes, sir, Chief Inspector." Jaouhari nodded.

"Now to make this more difficult," Kadiri paused and looked around. "Pull the sheets off the bed in here and in the Fielding's room. We'll cover Millie, her husband and each of the Fieldings with a single sheet, then rush them to the car. Once we arrive at the courthouse, we will do the same and rush them into the building."

Jaouhari nodded and picked up his phone. "I'll call two trusted men to get inside the courthouse and the chamber to be sure the rooms are clear." He dialed the call while Kadiri helped Millie pull the sheets from their bed, while the others followed suit in the Fieldings' room.

"Sir, my men tell me the Tribunal members are gathering in the courtroom now, Chief Inspector."

"Okay, we will leave quickly."

Kadiri gathered the sheet laden group at the door.

"You lead the way to the car, Senior Sergeant, I'll follow close behind." Kadiri opened the door and bolted into the hall. "All clear! Come now!"

Four shrouded figures waddled into the hall.

Jaouhari grabbed a hand of the first person, the others followed as he led them down the staircase. On the first floor, he moved to their side, guarding the spot most vulnerable to attack. Kadiri brought up the rear. They moved swiftly as a unit to the outside doors, Jaouhari pushed the doors open and herded the group toward the car. All four squeezed into the back seat.

Kadiri jumped behind the wheel, as Jaouhari filled the front passenger seat. Off they sped to the courthouse, arriving in seconds.

The surveillance team met them at the front doors. "All clear Senior Sergeant."

The four were hustled in again, like cattle.

Jaouhari headed straight to the private door of the rear chambers. As he passed, one of the men shoved an envelope into his hand, but he was too busy to stop.

Inside the chamber, Kadiri looked around. "The

windows are too high to be a threat and there are only two doors into this room. You guard the one we just came through, Jaouhari while I gather the Tribunal members."

Sheets began to be pulled off, but Kadiri turned and yelled, "Wait! Leave the sheets on. Remain covered."

The four obediently smoothed their sheets back into place as Kadiri opened the door to the members of the full Tribunal panel. "Gentlemen will you join us in Chambers please?"

A couple could be heard grumbling, but they entered as requested.

Jaouhari opened the envelope he had been handed and pulled out a multi-page report.

The Secretary-General scowled. "Why are these people wearing sheets over their heads? This is highly improper."

Kadiri addressed the judges. "Members of the Tribunal, thank you for your patience and cooperation. We have prepared a list for you of reasons why we believe Bryan Saunders is a criminal and should be taken into custody." He passed out four copies, one to each of the judges. "As you will see."

But the door behind Jaouhari creaked as it pushed slowly inwards. Bryan Saunders peered through the door. "Gentlemen, if you will excuse me, I am here to arrest the Secretary-General for numerous crimes including the theft of the Amelia Rose, being the one who issued the orders to have the crew set adrift and for issuing the order to murder Ferdinand Modesto."

The Secretary-General pulled an air-gun from beneath his robe and swung toward Saunders.

One of the sheets flew off and wrapped around his

arm, causing the dart to be entangled.

Three other sheets flew through the air as armed officers, charged the head tribunal member and cuffed him.

Kadiri turned to Jaouhari. “Thank you, Senior Sergeant, for trusting me and following my lead. I could not inform you in advance of the report I received last night from Interpol, I was afraid the room might be bugged. I saw you open the envelope I had arranged for you, so this did not come entirely as a surprise. Saunders had alerted the officials at Interpol to his suspicions, after realizing Mrs. Williams life had been threatened after each time he had alerted the Secretary-General of their schedule or her whereabouts. It seems that Interpol recruited one of your officers as an inside man to help Saunders, if he needed, so no need to prosecute your rebel officer.”

Jaouhari placed his hands on his hips. “I must admit, when four officers entered Mrs. Williams room from Dr. and Mrs. Fielding’s adjoining room, I was puzzled, but I had a peace in my spirit. And when they came in without saying a word, but holding their finger to their lips and took the sheets from the Williams’ and Fieldings’ I figured something special was happening.”

Kadiri nodded. “Ah, yes, that peace that passes all understanding.[vi] You can feel free now to call the officer who is guarding Mrs. Williams and her family. Tell them it is over and we will come take them to lunch and explain everything.”

Chapter 28

Lunch

Lunch took place at Dar Zellij,[vii] a local favorite restaurant in Marrakesh. Jaouhari recommended the Seffa, a dish of couscous or vermicelli noodles served with a sweet and savory onion sauce and chicken pieces topped with ground almonds, icing sugar and cinnamon.[viii]

Everyone ate to their capacity.

Millie leaned back on her cushion. “My goodness, I’m glad this is all over, but honestly Alif, I nearly had a heart attack when your soldiers came skulking into our room. For a moment, I thought you were the bad guy, then,” she tipped her eyes to the ceiling, “my commander placed His peace in my spirit, but poor George, I thought we were going to have to scoop him up off of the floor.” She glanced at her husband and laughed. “Serves you right, dear, for trying to *forbid* me to do something.”

Everyone laughed, but George.

His eyes stared at the table, then up at his wife. “Honestly, sweetheart, I was terrified that I would lose you if you tried to go to court again. I’m sorry I spoke so harshly to you, but I would have thrown myself in front of a tank if I had to, to keep you safe.”

She leaned toward him and stroked his face. "Oh, George, I love you so much."

Abby chimed in. "Once you and your four sheet-covered men were gone, Chief Inspector, the worse part for me was having to be silent until you called. You know, it was like needing to scratch an itch when you're supposed to be still and I thought of so many things I needed to tell Millie, George and Sam."

He chuckled. "But you all played your parts marvelously. My sentry told me you were all very still and quiet. If the room contained a listening device and if the Secretary-General had been listening, he would have known instantly that something was wrong. He might have tried to flee and we might never have caught him. As it stands now, Saunders who is on his way to London with the former Secretary-General in cuffs and under heavy guard. You all are to be commended," then he turned his gaze to Jaouhari, "and the Senior Sergeant will be granted a promotion due to his stellar handling of this matter."

George stuck his hand toward the Senior Sergeant. "Congratulations, Jaouhari."

Millie leaned her head on George's shoulder. "Can we go back to the ship now, dear?"

George withdrew his hand and cradled his wife. "Indeed, we can, dearest. Chief Inspector Kadiri has offered to escort us to Tangier Med to meet the ship."

"Can we invite him aboard for dinner, George?"

"Anything you wish, my dear." And he sealed it with a kiss.

The End!

June Whatley has taught first through third grades in a Christian school; she has also taught Middle Graders in two different Christian schools; and has taught Study Skills in the Remedial Developmental Department of the third largest college in Tennessee.

Mrs. Whatley holds a combination Master of Arts degree in Counseling and Education from Regent University in Virginia Beach, Virginia.

June is a wife, mother and grandmother of four of the greatest Grands in history.

---

[i] https://en.wikipedia.org/wiki/Al-Boraq

[ii] https://theculturetrip.com/africa/morocco/articles/the-best-street-food-in-marrakech/

[iii] Musixmatch, Songwriters, J. Kennedy/H. Williams, Red Sails in the Sunset lyrics, Peter Maurice Music Co Ltd.

Endnotes

[iv] Isa 54:17.

[v] Psa 91:10-11.

[vi] Philippians 4:7.

[vii] https://theculturetrip.com/africa/morocco/articles/10-moroccan-restaurants-that-are-some-of-the-worlds-best-ever/

[viii] http://www.mymoroccanfood.com/home/seffa-moroccan-chicken-with-vermicelli

hariua

Made in the USA
Middletown, DE
23 April 2022

64531276R00089